DESERTER

Gambling, tank towns, always on the move — that was Bart Laish's life. Sometimes he told himself it was no good, but it was in his blood and he knew he couldn't change.

He'd tried before. There was West Point, and they'd thrown him out. He'd signed on as a line trooper, but the old fever was still there, and one night in a dice game he'd started a riot that meant the guardhouse.

So now he was on the run again — a deserter with a price on his head and too many ready to collect it. He rode on through the dust until he thought he saw a way — a burned-out camp, and a dying general with news of a wagon train ahead. Maybe in a general's uniform that train could get Laish to Oregon.

But when he caught up with it, he found the odds were a thousand vengeance-crazed Indians against 70 fumbling recruits. . . and a woman who didn't care what he was — as long as he was hers.

ARROW

An original novel — not a reprint

in the DUST

● By L. L. FOREMAN

A DELL FIRST EDITION

Published by
DELL PUBLISHING COMPANY, INC.
261 Fifth Avenue
New York 16, New York

Copyright, 1954,
by L. L. Foreman

A short version of this novel was published in
Zane Grey's Western under the title, PLATTE
RIVER GAMBLE

Library of Congress Catalog Card No. 53-13262

Designed and produced by
Western Printing & Lithographing Company

Cover painting by Robert Stanley

Printed In U. S. A.

CHAPTER 1

HE WAS A SOLITARY CAVALRYMAN riding westward into the empty land toward the setting sun. His tunic was faded, discolored with dried mud and split down the back from some past act of exertion. The breeches, of lighter blue, had worn threadbare at the knees. The bandanna knotted around his neck was a dirty yellow rag.

He looked used up rather than slovenly, like a man who hadn't had time lately to look after himself. The hard gauntness of his unshaven face betrayed fatigue and lost sleep, but no loss of tough tenacity.

The trail bent around a long limestone shelf. He kept his eyes front until he rounded in sight of the lonely roadhouse huddled under the shelf, and after paying it a rapid inspection he looked back over his route. His trail from the east, as far as he could see, lay as godforsakenly empty as the land on the west of the roadhouse. It would be dark pretty soon. He pushed on to the roadhouse and rode around to the back. Dismounting stiffly, he pressed his hands against the small of his back while listening to the murmur of voices from inside. Nobody came out.

For the sake of the horse he was tempted to throw the saddle off, but it wouldn't do. He compromised by hefting the saddle and airing it, and leaving it on the horse, loose-girthed. When he paced around to the front, he took a moment to peer in through the window. Then he shoved open the door and entered, inhaling the familiar smells of strong tobacco and whisky and human beings.

He bought a drink and carried it to a corner table where he could sit with his back to the wall. His business was urgent, but he couldn't rush it. The place was a boars'-nest, a bit below average even for a frontier grogshop. The proprietor, who said his name was Owsley, might or might not co-operate.

This was his last chance. He swallowed his drink and leaned back, waiting to catch Owsley's eye. It felt good to sit still and relax for a little while.

It was late May, 1869, the time of year when westward traffic had dwindled to the summer slump. The emigrant wagon trains had gone rolling off on schedule, most of them a month ago, to reach and cross the faraway Rockies before the September onset of mountain snows. Peace reigned on the plains this year, according to the Indian Bureau and the Washington reports, so there were no military movements of much consequence on the great trails westward.

So Owsley's roadhouse was slack for trade even now at sundown, being situated west beyond the Bull Creek turn-off to that long, long haul to Oregon. Hell knew what Owsley did for business when the trail running past his place stayed deserted for weeks at a stretch. In all likelihood, the trooper thought, hell certainly did know.

In the barroom half a dozen drunken frontier tramps were scraping up the price of another bottle. There was an emaciated old Pawnee who listened ponderingly to their loose talk and mumbled to himself once in a while. And there was an incredibly ragged boy trying to beg a penny.

The boy couldn't have been more than twelve, and he

6

had a lot to learn about begging. After trying to touch the tramps, he got around to asking, "Got a copper you can spare, sojer?" He didn't sound very hopeful. Young as he was he knew troopers notoriously blew their thirteen dollars a month on pay night and scrabbled for coppers themselves the rest of the time.

And this trooper bore particular signs of having traveled a long and tough trail from his last pay. But he raised his head when the tramps laughed at the boy. His hard face flared with sudden irritation. The cold sweep of his eyes silenced their laugh. They saw then that he had the stamp of a sharp-edged man, and they withdrew their attention.

To the boy he said, "No folks?"

The boy shook his head dumbly. Owsley, hearing the question, called quietly from behind the bar, "Cholera."

The soldier nodded, without any softening of expression, and took off his dusty campaign hat and dropped it to the floor beside his chair. His hair was the color of tarnished old brass; to the boy he was suddenly a blond Satan, callous and sinister. He slipped a hand under his torn tunic, where a button was missing, as if to scratch himself. The boy turned hopelessly away, but a tiny clink of coins jerked him around. The fishing hand had reappeared with a gold double-eagle held between long forefinger and thumb.

"For luck, kid," came the murmur, dry and unsentimental.

The boy's eyes bugged. Fearful of a mistake, or a cruel joke, he snatched the gold piece and ran. At the door he flung a glance backward. Nobody was after him. The shabby trooper sat looking across the barroom at Owsley in a curiously inquiring manner.

Thoughtfully Owsley began lighting up the lamps. He

7

brought one, and a drink, over to the corner table. "On the house," he said. He had a trick of holding in his lips when he spoke, and the look in his hooded black eyes drifted everywhere but at the trooper. "That twenty dollars for luck says you're a gambling man. Me too. I'll lay long odds you're over the hill."

There was no response. "I spotted you for one, soon's I saw you ride up. It's something no sloper can hide, long's he wears the harness. Even the kid guessed it. What do I call you?"

"Laish."

"You're unusual. Not Smith, and not broke." Owsley dipped a look at the empty buttonhole, a look that searched for the bulge of a money belt. "Laish—what can I sell you? I can supply any man with anything in reason, if he can pay for it."

"I can pay—in reason. I need clothes, pack horse, outfit and supplies for the trail. I've got a good riding horse."

"The long jump, eh? Man, you *do* need luck!"

Laish finished his drink. "When did the last wagon train go through west?"

"Week before last," Owsley told him. "Emigrant outfit. Cholera held it up, back in the settlements. Like to never got off at all, but Tillotson—the Green River trader —he joined in with his freight wagons and crew, and they 'lected him captain. Something had held him up too. He'll keep them emigrants humpin', to make up time. You better let me fix you a place to hole up till—"

"No," Laish said. "I'll try catching up with that emigrant train. For my health it's Oregon or bust."

"Well, it's your affair. I wonder, though, you didn't strike for Santa Fe on the south trail. It's a hell-sight closer. Santa Fe's where they mostly head for when the law lights a fire. She's a real fragrant ripper of a town, I hear."

"My inclinations," Laish said, "bent that way. I had Old Mexico in mind. But back there at Bull Creek I learned that the patrols are out as far as Council Grove and maybe even farther. So it's Oregon."

"Can't double back, eh? You must've skinned the brigade paymaster!"

Having finally pooled enough to buy a bottle, the tramps set up a banging clamor at the bar. Owsley went to serve them.

He brought back another drink for Laish, a stiff one to put him in the mood to stick around and spend his money. "I never try to change a man's mind. But here's something you ought to know. Couple days back, a bowlegs general came through here—name of Pepperis. He's bound west for Fort Laramie with an escort of juniper doughfoots on horseback. Fact! As I get it, he's on orders to take over command at Laramie. His first call's Fort Taylor, which can't be much, because them Johnny Raws only went out there this spring. Guess he'll pick up a fresh escort there and push on to Laramie. You better stop here a while, I'm telling you."

Once or twice it had occurred to Laish that perhaps he was a trifle careless—that perhaps some caution might forestall the unexpected complications that frequently confronted him. But gambling and a talent for violence, plus a taste for fast and untamed company, were somehow always in the way of these sober thoughts.

He set his emptied glass down with a snap, the only betrayal of his feelings. General Pepperis, eh? Brigadier General Andrew Wyatt Pepperis. Pepper Andy.

"Did he have a supply wagon and ambulance along with him?" he queried. And, at Owsley's nod, he commented wryly, "At his rate of travel, then, he'll be between me and that wagon train clear to Laramie. It's damn small chance I've got of getting past him."

Owsley eyed him curiously, caught by something in his tone. "Does that general know you by sight?"

The only response from Laish was a brief rise and fall of his hand on the table. His eyes narrowed a fraction and some inner humor brought a faint change to the line of his lips. He asked, with an odd drag of reluctance, "Is his wife with him? If it's a permanent change of station—"

"Oh, she went through—let's see, now—must be a month past," Owsley answered. "She joined the last train ahead of Tillotson's. Lot more comfortable for her, I guess. There was a doctor and his daughter in that train, and she made friends with 'em. They traveled together. Her own kind of people—know what I mean? Damn pretty woman, the general's wife. Young, too. I never saw a prettier woman."

Laish nodded musingly, and the line of his lips softly gentled. Then that was gone in the alert upswing of his head as the door of the barroom banged open suddenly.

It was the ragged boy who rushed in. He yelled to Laish, "Sojers coming!"

Laish caught up his hat and was instantly around the table and leaping to the door. It was dark outside now. The opened door and a window poked bright holes into the night. He pulled the door shut behind him and stood against it a moment until the trail from the east came up as a pallid glimmer and he saw the cavalry detail—four troopers and a noncom in the lead—jogging so terribly close to the roadhouse that his ears caught the faint slap of their saber scabbards.

He swung swiftly away from the door, but the lighted window betrayed the familiar yellow stripe down his breeches. The sedate jog of the cavalry detail broke at once, quickening, and there came a shout of, "Hey, you!"

—followed by a harsh and throaty *"Halt!"*

The noncom must have been carrying his carbine loose in the boot for him to get it up so fast. It crashed a report right at the tail-end of his command. At the dark corner of the roadhouse Laish whirled, lifted his heavy Colt's gun, and laid two shots well below the flash of the carbine. His efficiency with a gun matched his cleverness at cards, as a certain guardhouse captain had once observed.

The foremost horse floundered headlong, and the noncom catapulted a complete and beautiful gilhooley. Laish knew that fellow by his voice: a rook-riding sergeant who one day had decided to hand him a pasting behind the stables, and had come to later in the infirmary, swearing Laish had clubbed him. That had meant the guardhouse for Laish.

Laish sprinted on around to his horse. Lacking time to tighten girth, he legged into the saddle, toed in tight, and took off westward, minus outfit and supplies for the long jump.

Positively his health required that far-off Oregon climate. He wondered if he'd ever get there.

CHAPTER 2

By the third day out he was in a black temper. He had shot a cow that had escaped its emigrant owner, so he was not hungry. But without salt, beef was not satisfying. And there was no coffee nor tobacco.

To avoid the notice of any Indian parties on the prowl, he traveled at night and lay low wherever he could by day. It was wise, but he didn't like it.

That day, camped in a willow patch by a water hole, he witnessed a scene that left him with an odd sense of foreboding. He had never by choice been a plainsman. His preference ran to roaring mining camps and the wide-open towns of the cattle trails. But he knew that prairie wolves were an unusual sight here at this season, and it made him uneasy to watch a lean mob of them hounding a buffalo bull.

The wolves raced with the shaggy buffalo, snapping at it. They fed on him as they ran, every snap of their teeth tearing off flesh. By the time they brought him to earth his hind quarters were bone, and then they all piled into him. Nice country.

In places the great trail spread a half-mile wide, a myriad of deep wheel tracks. This was caused by wagoners pulling out of previous tracks for fear of bogging hub-deep in the earth, made spongy by spring rains. For a horseman the course was not too difficult. Laish rode alongside the gigantic muddy scar, always on watch. Somewhere on ahead traveled General Pepperis, a cavalry martinet with hawk eyes and an infallible memory.

There was grass in abundance, but the bay horse missed its grain ration. There was also plenty of water. The country was soaked. On the seventh night a gully-washing rain roared down, to disprove the persistent fallacy that April's end marked the beginning of summer drought on the plains. Finding no shelter, Laish and the bay bowed heads to the storm and slogged on through the night.

"Twelve o'clock and all's wet!" Laish muttered, shivering, trying to fire up a sense of humor that had always been essentially dry.

Toward dawn he came upon the general's last camp.

Due to the darkness and the leaden screen of the downpour, the camp simply emerged quite suddenly. He rode right into it. He saw the grayish-white blur of the supply wagon to his left. The oblong shape of the general's own ambulance showed just ahead, small by comparison. No fire; this rainstorm was enough to quench the furnaces of hell.

Motionless and alert on the halted bay, he waited to hear the startled challenge of a sentry. There wasn't a sound apart from the lashing rain and the occasional crash of thunder. As his peering eyes unraveled the gloom he saw with a hammering shock that this was literally the general's last camp.

The canvas top of the supply wagon flapped raggedly, ripped by looting hands. The ambulance lay overturned, its team and driver heaped in a dead tangle. There was this and more for Laish to see when he pushed farther into it.

"God!" he muttered.

He swung down to the ground and steadied the bay, the animal snorting and shooting its ears at three long shapes sprawled together in the littered debris from the wagon. Other such shapes were isolated humps in the grass here and there.

He tied the stamping bay to a wheel of the wagon, and made a brief scout on foot. Feeling over the ground around the dead men, he could find only a few empty cartridge shells. The scattered positions of the bodies, too, indicated little organized resistance, no tight stand at all. He remembered Owsley's description of the general's escort as juniper doughfoots on horseback—infantry recruits mounted temporarily, very temporarily. They had ridden unaware into action, their one and only fight, before they were anywhere near trained ready for it. And the general, Pepper Andy, who had seen action enough for forty men in his time, had ridden into it with them and got it, evidently as unsuspecting as they.

Laish considered the sour prospect of burial for the dead while he tramped around in the rain searching for the general. The Indians had carried off their own dead, if any, as their custom ruled. It was not very sensible, he reflected, that the people of most races felt impelled to tender respectful rites to the corpses of their fellows who in life probably never merited more than casual attention.

As he searched, pondering, he heard in the muffling downpour a gasping, grumbling kind of sound. He was passing the ambulance and it seemed to come out of there. At once he drew his gun and crouched stockstill, listening. The grumble came again, and now he recognized it as the swearing of a hurt and angry man.

He stepped quickly to the rear end of the overturned ambulance. One canvas flap hung almost straight. The other

14

dangled sodden and askew in the mud.

Careful not to poke his head in abruptly, he inquired, "General Pepperis?" Wounded men fired at anything, if able, like injured animals blindly striking and kicking the rescuer, like a bogged steer charging the cowpuncher who roped it out.

The reply came, though, in a tone of quiet moderation. "Yes. Come in. Who are you?"

"Private Turley, sir," said Laish, giving his Army name, and crawled in. "Ninth Cavalry." It wasn't light enough for the general to see him clearly.

"Well, damn me!" exclaimed the general tiredly. "Where in hell did you come from? Any more with you?"

"No, sir." Laish knelt by him.

"You a courier?"

There it was, the inevitable questioning to ascertain the status of a lone trooper three hundred miles out from the settlements and a far cry more than that from his post. Dying, the general could yet fasten his inspection on an irregularity.

"No, sir."

And that, bare of any explanation, stood as an admission of criminal guilt.

General Pepperis asked no further questions. He lay against the ribs of the ambulance, his eyes shining coldly, in a tangle of bedding and camp gear that had evidently buried him when the vehicle capsized.

Among what was left of the jumbled contents of the ambulance Laish unearthed a pint-sized, leather-covered canteen. The fact that the Indians had overlooked it was a sign of their haste. He unscrewed the stopper, sniffed whisky, and with a gently lifting arm he got Pepperis into position to drink without choking.

On the second swallow Pepperis hacked a cough and

pushed the canteen away. He lay back again then, silently contemplating the graying patch of sky visible through the rear of the ambulance, as if weighing and tabulating in his mind all that had happened for his official report.

The rain let up just as the sun rimmed the east, and there was the fresh land rolling in folds to the blue sky. Light struck directly into the ambulance, showing Pepperis to be a haggardly severe-featured man of large size, whose eyes at this moment were as blank of expression as the star on his shoulder.

At last the general said, "You've aged a good deal, Bart. That doesn't surprise me, considering the life you've led. There's quite a difference in our ages, as I recall, but you look as old as I do."

Laish drew a long, slow breath. In this fresh light of dawn his eyes were pale agate framed in dark shadows of sunken sockets. He felt old.

He said, lying, "*You* hold your age well. Any man who has fought the Apaches and the Sioux and served his country as long as you have, Andy, might be expected to look older."

Pepperis shifted his eyes and looked straight at him. "How would you know that?" he asked. And when Laish failed to reply, he said, "You've come a long way, Bart, in seven years. A long way down. Gambler—gunfighter—outlaw! And now an army deserter! How much farther can you go?"

"To Oregon," Laish said soberly. "Nobody knows me there."

"God help Oregon," muttered General Pepperis.

Together in the cramped quarters of the overturned ambulance, the general and the deserter listened to the utter silence all around them.

Although the early sun was warming the air, Laish shivered in his wet clothes. It was not true, surely, that he had aged so much beyond his years. The tough times recently had scored their marks on him; nothing that couldn't be cured. Pepperis didn't realize how ancient *he* looked this bright morning, and he was past cure.

Laish tipped the canteen of whisky and drank from it, and as he brought it down he heard a murmur from Pepperis:

"That wasn't what set you off—the drinking. You can't use that excuse. No, it was the restless streak. You always had it. That wild streak that you never would try to hold under control. Undisciplined!"

And that fell short of the whole truth, too. But nothing could be gained by arguing against it. Laish would not deny him whatever satisfaction he could find in laying the blame on natural cussedness. Most likely, he thought, behind these condemning words the general fended off his own remembrance of a West Pointer headlong in love with a girl from Charleston, years ago, and the dashing major who stepped in and changed the picture.

"Discipline," Laish said, in concession, "always came pretty hard to me, Andy. How is Mignon?" A lovely and slightly absurd name, he had always thought it: the kind of name that was in fashion in the South, among the old families.

"She is well, I believe."

He nodded, sorry that he had asked. The stiff reticence of the general's reply confirmed the Army gossip about his married life. Perhaps it explained why such an ambitious soldier, headed straight for a high career at Department, had chosen to become a grim and rather plodding field officer forever pulling wires to get himself ordered out on still another campaign and another long tour of duty. As a major, on West Point staff, he had enjoyed a dazzling prestige and been given to considerable swank. He had embellished everything he touched with his vigorous personality. It had not seemed out of line then for him to win and wed a girl who was young enough to be his daughter.

As a brigadier general in the field he was a taciturn old bowlegs, sour old soldier. Plain Pepper Andy, nemesis of recalcitrant Red Men, and the nightmare of Junior officers.

"We all have to pay our toll, one way or other, whichever way we go," Pepperis said, and it sounded likely that he spoke as much for himself as for Laish, until he added, "You chose your own road."

"I chose it," Laish agreed. There had been an alternative, not suited to his temper. "I've never tried to excuse it, even to myself. I wouldn't begin now, to you. Why preach? You must have a reason."

Pepperis half lowered his eyelids and changed the subject. "It wasn't the Sioux this time. Nor Apaches."

He stuck up a bony finger and named them. "Pawnees, Crows, Shoshones. Some Sacs and Foxes. They rode right at us as we broke camp. No circling. Not one hostile sign. Not a single shot till they closed in. It didn't last three minutes then. They rode on west, I think. I don't know how long I was out. Not long. I heard them leaving. Why do you suppose they did it?"

Laish rolled a shoulder. The whisky hit his stomach and he began feeling more like himself—a man who took a skeptical view of what most other men judged to be success and failure. He was able to see the irony of the string of circumstances that had brought him onto this trail, following unwillingly the two persons whom he had gone so far to avoid so long ago. One here, the other waiting ahead at Fort Laramie.

"The celebrated element of sheer Indian cussedness seems to me sufficient explanation for—"

"You're a hell of a soldier!" Pepperis interrupted acridly. "It's damn little you know about these Plains Indians. These tribes out here don't band up together like that unless they've got a definite objective. Pawnees, Crows, Shoshones—this wasn't any wildcat impulse. The whole nature of the attack disproves it."

More softly, he said, "They were led by Rasakura, a Pawnee chief. Rasakura served under me as chief of scouts against Red Cloud's Sioux. I gave him a silver medal. Big handsome devil. He still wore the medal. He shot me and my driver, and then the rest cut loose. I wasn't expecting that."

Stretching his legs out, he sighed deeply, not as a man in pain, but as one bitterly aware of his inability to cope with a disastrous situation. During most of his career in the saddle he had fought from the Mexican border up to the Yellowstone. Out of the saddle he had struggled with red tape, false economies, and impossible orders from higher up. He was not a brilliant campaigner, but he had a flare for getting things done in some fashion or other. It was his quality of dogged persistence, which from afar off passed for shining ability and even a touch of genius, that had earned him his brigadier's star in a scrimped skeleton of an army where sixty-year-old captains were not uncommon.

Laish moved restlessly, squatting on his heels. He said, "There's an emigrant train late out—" and left the rest unfinished.

"I know." The general slowly turned bitter eyes to him. "You begin to see, do you? That logically is their main objective, assuming that they have one. Their method is to cut off all aid and communication—close the trail behind it. Then the massing of forces. A series of raids and attacks, to cripple it. Finally the grand kill, and the—er— fruits of victory enjoyed at their leisure. No doubt there's the usual mob of women and children in that emigrant train."

Cold-bloodedly he added, "It's not a new pattern. It is old and effective. All it requires is deliberate organization. That comes harder to the Indian than it does to us, but he can do it when he thinks the prize is worth it. There's little else we can teach him about the game."

Casting up an estimate, Laish spoke of Fort Taylor. "The train should be somewhere in that vicinity by now. It'll have protection."

"Fort Taylor!" snorted the general. "A street of tents on the open prairie! Garrisoned with infantry recruits and green officers never west of the Mississippi before this spring! Back at Fort Gibson they were given horses for the march, left by a disbanded cavalry outfit. Not one in three of them could ride! My escort had to be made up from the sick-list they left behind there at Gibson! By God, does Department think we're on a picnic out here?"

Getting no reply to that from Laish, he demanded brusquely, "You got a good horse?" And at Laish's nod, he commented, "I might know you would! Your colonel's, probably!"

"No. The captain's was the better mount."

For a moment it seemed that General Pepperis was about to display his right to his Pepper Andy nickname. He controlled his anger, and then his stare became withdrawn and masked in thought.

Presently he said, "It's a toss-up whether Rasakura's pack will attack Fort Taylor. Depends on how big they rate their medicine, after fixing me. They might by-pass it, to catch the wagon train farther on. In the sandhills, say, along the Platte. Any case, Taylor is the only hope for those people—if the train is Rasakura's objective, and I think it is. Yes."

The "Yes" meant that he had reached and confirmed a decision. "My writing-case is somewhere in this mess," he told Laish. "Find it, please, and write out a dispatch to Major Wycoff, commanding Fort Taylor. My orders are as follows: He will immediately abandon Taylor, destroying such equipment and supplies as cannot be conveniently moved out. He will proceed to the emigrant train, wherever it may be, and escort it to Fort Laramie."

Laish began searching for the writing-case, then paused. Softly, brutally, he inquired, "And who will carry that dispatch?"

"You will," replied Pepperis, just as softly. "I'm making you a soldier, Cousin Bart, for the good of your soul!"

"Very kind of you," Laish murmured. He knelt in the jumble and considered it aloud. "A hundred miles of trail, watched by hostiles all out to keep it closed. Fort Taylor probably under attack. If I make it, I'm stuck with that Taylor garrison. And if I live to reach Fort Laramie—"

"They'll throw you in the guardhouse," Pepperis finished for him, in a voice that sounded far away. "Oh, you'll cook up a plausible story, sure. They won't swallow it. Any stable dog can spot you for what you are. But you're going to do this, just the same."

"You think so?"

"I know so." The trembling hollows on each side of the general's mouth made him appear to be grinning sardonically. "Women and children in that emigrant train, remember—or have you changed so much?"

"Not that much, Andy."

"I didn't think you had, Bart. I didn't think you could. And say—if you do get to Fort Laramie, tell Mignon. Tell her I hoped it would work. A permanent station, I mean. Lonely there. It might have drawn us together again, after all. I was ready to try damned hard, tell her."

"I'll tell her."

"Don't waste time on any burying around here," Pepperis said. "Get that paper—hurry! I'll sign it."

But he didn't sign it. He was dead the next minute, before Laish could find the writing-case.

Laish squatted there a long time in the silent ambulance. He looked about him, his glance touching on the general's broken camp box, the upset bedding and gear, a few books. Lastly he looked down into the stilled face, the face of a hardworking old soldier whose final concern had been to project his authority beyond his death, for the welfare of some people he had never known and never seen.

A minute—a few dozen lost heartbeats—had canceled out the general's last order. A written dispatch was worthless without his distinctive signature.

It was perhaps possible to get through to Fort Taylor and swear to the general's orders, yes. There was no possibility whatever that Major Wycoff or any other commander would abandon his post on the word of a stray trooper, let alone a deserter. To do so would lay him open to certain court-martial later.

No. Being fresh to the West, and therefore probably scornful of Indian fighting ability, Major Wycoff would go by the book. Send forth half his company of mounted infantry to protect the wagon train. Stand by with the other half at the Fort.

The Indians would be delighted, if they were out in force for business. Experts at warfare, they knew the counter-move to that gambit. First the surprise attack on the little garrison at dawn. Then on to the wagon train, the main objective, as Pepperis had called it.

And he—Laish—if he got through, would be one of the beans in that Fort Taylor bake-pot.

One by one he reviewed all aspects of the matter, much as he would have sized up the possibilities and percentages of a poker hand. It kept recurring to him that Major Wycoff and his company were new to the West, that in all likelihood none of them knew General Pepperis by sight. This, his hunch told him, was an ace if he could figure out how to use it. He studied it and let it sink deep in his mind while he squatted by the body of the general.

The instant he found himself blankly contemplating the star on the general's shoulder, he had the solution and it was simple.

In ten minutes he stood straight and tall at the open tail of the ambulance, dressed in the general's uniform, wearing the general's saber, the front brim of the black campaign hat creased upward in rakish cavalry style. All he lacked was the general's drooping daggers of mustaches, practically required dress for a regular cavalryman. He would, he thought humorlessly, set a new fashion.

For a minute longer he stood looking at the body in the ambulance. With a self-consciousness that was rare in him, he saluted it hurriedly before turning away. It was not too smartly clipped a salute, for his Army time had run to only a few weeks, during which he had managed to avoid all but a bare minimum of drill. He had no liking for discipline, as he had admitted to Pepperis. As for West Point, the details of that previous term of servitude were long sloughed off and deliberately forgotten.

In no way did the life of a rooky yellowlegs suit his temperament. They even wanted to change his free-and-easy style of riding a horse. He did not see fit to compromise, because it didn't seem worth while. His enlistment had been merely a covering of his tracks, a dodge into temporary anonymity made necessary by certain events not far behind him and catching up at the time. It had turned out to be even more temporary than he had expected.

He strode to the bay horse, untied it and mounted, and rode away over the gently undulating ground whose green-spangled grass now glittered in the sunlight, heading westward. Half a mile off he reigned the horse full around to a halt, for a last look at the shambles.

All around the scene of the attack lay the endless, motionless prairie. The ambulance and supply wagon and bodies were nothing but a small cluster of casual objects, like a patch of wreckage on the open sea.

Only then did a slow thud of wrath punch into him. The muscles of his stomach tightened, while he got a sudden fancy of that forlorn scene multiplied: two score or more wrecked wagons, two hundred or more bodies, women and children among them.

He swore an immoderate oath, swung the horse around, and rode on.

CHAPTER 3

A<small>T A DISTANCE</small> Fort Taylor resembled a giant's distraction with elemental geometry executed in charcoal. Smeared circles, squares, oblongs; they crowded one another in a thin, dirty haze. On closer inspection the smearedness proved more pronounced, the geometric figures more fuzzy, till finally the whole thing was just a hodge-podge, the burned-out remains of a place recently inhabited by men.

Tracks cutting out from it told the story. Reading what he could of it, Laish surmised that at least part of the garrison had broken out and dashed westward with two or three wagons. The wagons would be for their wounded, and for carrying along some supplies and ammunition. The tracks of unshod ponies, Indian tracks, were everywhere around. The bay horse snuffed and snorted uneasily.

"Smell 'em, do you? Or is it the smoke?" Laish absently scratched the animal's neck. This now was dry country. No rain had fallen to damp out the smoking ashes. The horse would soon be needing water, and so would he. This smoke was no help.

He hawked and spat. All day he had been striking the tracks of Indian parties, every one of them converging on to the main trail, and every one of them pointing west. It was not unduly pessimistic to suppose that those parties were hurrying to join Rasakura's main band. The general's judgment stood supported. Here was organized purpose, aimed at a definite objective.

It was difficult to imagine this place as, yesterday or the day before, a tidy military camp—well-aligned tents glittering boldly in the strong light, stables and company office smelling pleasantly of new lumber; men in uniforms not yet faded, booting through the monotonous routines at the summons of a bugle.

This was what happened when the tribes dropped their differences and concentrated upon destruction. Those green troops had got a terrible lesson, and no doubt were still getting it somewhere. Rasakura's band must by now have grown to tremendous strength. Not many travois drag marks, so they had few women along. War-parties, all of them.

Squinting under eyelids half shuttered against the late afternoon sun, Laish raised his glance to the trail ahead, then sent it on a reaching sweep around to settle eventually on a tiny bloom of dust in the northeast.

"And still they come," he murmured. "How right you were, Andy! The country's swarming with them."

It was not in his nature to let himself get stampeded. The coolly estimated percentage and the calculated chance were taproots of his gambler's training. He took the time to throw off the saddle, to air and smooth the saddle blanket, and when he was ready to go he gave another glance to the dust cloud. It was bigger, nearer. Their sharp eyes had spotted him, of course. They were after him.

Rasakura's medicine had proved big. Fort Taylor had fallen and its garrison commander did not require any general to order him out after the emigrant train. Laish felt somewhat orphaned, but there remained only one remedy for it and that was to follow the derelict garrison.

The sun had less than two hours to go. He figured he could stay ahead of the dust cloud that long and still conserve the bay for a run in the dark.

Against the night's blackness the fires of the Indian camps rimmed a mile of the prairie in smoky pink. Curved in a great arc, the camps stood as a bracket that blocked the wagon train from eastern retreat, by day pushing forward in that same order like a line of hunters relentlessly driving the prey on toward a ground chosen for the kill.

By shuttering his eyelids to cut down the fire-glare, Laish was able to make out a continual ant-like activity. With half a dozen or more tribes represented there, much visiting was going on. Isolated fires dotted the two horns of the arc, and from them riders raced out openly in twos and threes and returned from circling wide around the wagon train, two miles farther on. A never-ending hubbub boomed, interspersed now and then by the thin yell of some exuberant brave mad with anticipation.

The time, Laish guessed, was drawing near. Perhaps tomorrow. Their bold insolence in camping so close to the wagon train, and riding watch around it, was a measure of their contempt for the train's ability to defend itself.

For some time he held the bay at halt in the darkness, south of the trail and the Indian encampments. He moved on then at a walk, pistol in hand for emergency, watching for riders. A pair of them passed within a quarter-mile of him. He failed to see them till they dashed between him and the distant campfires. They appeared suddenly out of the black night and were gone. That added to his caution and he veered a bit farther out.

The big canvas tops of the wagons loomed up, pale, a great ring of them drawn in the fort-in pattern. He thought he saw the faint reflection of a shielded fire inside the hollow ring, but all was still and quiet.

It was striking, the contrast between this fateful silence and the drumming hullabaloo at the Indian fires. These were the prey, they the hunters. Tomorrow in the dust and sweat there would be cruelly frayed nerves to pay for this all-night vigil in the caravan. The lumbering, hopeless flight of the wagons might well break into panic. The Indians knew the game.

Laish reined in to listen and to get himself set for the fast run. The constant roar from the Indian camps made it difficult to distinguish any individual sound. It tricked the ear with a reverberating rhythm. Then a lean and half-naked rider flashed darkly across the intervening space, between him and the wagons, and the rhythm broke for that moment. After the rider grew tiny, Laish spurred and the bay lunged forward and rocked into full gallop.

He was abruptly aware of two more riders, ahead and on his left, rushing at him. They uttered no sound, but both executed a swift flurry of movement that fetched up two dull glimmers of metal.

He reined hard over to the left, dropping back from between them and the distant fires, and then he was broadside to them. For an instant he had a better sight of them than they had of him. They were between him and the distant rim of campfires. The Colt blared in his right hand.

The nearest pony took an enormous jump and came down on rubber legs, sprawled out. Its rider bounded clear, landing on his feet with barely a stumble. Momentarily unsure of his bearings and of Laish's movements, the unhorsed warrior crouched tautly, swinging his feathered head far over in search. His shining body split the rim of light. Laish fired at that standing target and saw it jerk and twist.

The other buck screwed around on his pony and got off a shot and howled furiously. He continued the howl without change of pitch after the next bullet from the heavy Colt smashed into him.

Laish lined out the bay fast for the wagons. They bulked up before him and still he saw and heard no sign of life among them. Then a gun flashed, close down, from a rifle pit, and he sang out to the nervous, unseen shooter, "Hold it, damn you—I'm coming in!"

The bay jumped the narrow rifle pit and beat on between wagons and beyond, where Laish reined in among a group of dim figures that closed in and crowded around him. Somebody grasped his bridle and demanded to know who he was and where he came from. Laish growled indistinctly and let the man guide him forward through teams of oxen, mules, past picket lines of horses. A squad trooped along behind him, without any sort of order.

He had been right about there being a sheltered fire inside the wagon corral. It was screened by boxes and bales, and inside this space was also a lighted lantern. Several men lay and sat on the ground. A glance told him that these were some of the wounded, the day's fresh casualties. A corporal with his right eye bandaged was helping a girl bind up the leg of a trooper. There was an open case of surgical instruments, a small heap of bloodstained rags, and a basin filled with pinkish, milky-looking water. And a smell of iodine and caustic, and drying blood and men's sweat.

The girl worked efficiently, and she did not look up. She had light brown hair, thick and curling, tied back at the nape of her neck with a strip torn from a red handkerchief. Laish couldn't see her face, bent over her task.

His guide was a sergeant, a man whose settled expression of dour skepticism marked him unmistakably as an old soldier. He had a crooked blue scar on his broken nose, and eyebrows so pale they were invisible. A deep discontent lay in his eyes like pain. Catching the sergeant staring thunderstruck at the brigadier's star on his shoulder, Laish remembered just in time not to ask him companionably how he was doing.

Abruptly the sergeant snapped to attention, brought to his senses by the hurried entrance of a lieutenant.

"Sergeant! Who the devil—!"

The lieutenant bit it off and he, too, stared incredulously at the brigadier's star. He was unable to hold down a queer noise in his throat, but he came smartly to attention and saluted. "Lieutenant King, sir."

"Pepperis," Laish said deliberately, returning the salute.

The girl raised her head. She had very clear eyes that gazed wonderingly at him, and she looked like every girl he had ever known and yet not a bit like any one of them. There was something about her that held him silent until she again bowed her head over the wounded trooper. And even then he kept looking down at her, until conscious that the lieutenant and the sergeant were waiting for him to speak.

They were an amazed pair, bursting to ask questions. Even so, the lieutenant's eyes for a bare instant reflected an emotion that was altogether different; it was a personal and quite man-to-man thing edged with guarded intolerance. Laish gave it a thought and guessed he had looked at the girl too long for the young officer's peace of mind. So it stood that way? Well.

Laish asked him quietly, properly, "Lieutenant, what have you to tell me?"

The guardedly intolerant look had vanished. "I regret to inform you of the loss of Major Wycoff, sir," Lieutenant King replied. "Also Captain Spencer and Captain

Beauford, and—"

"Are you left in command?"

"Yes, sir."

The melancholy discontent of the sergeant became at once understandable and revealing. This scene was enough to make angels weep.

For this Lieutenant King was very young and very green, with West Point written all over him and the ink not yet dry. Trained to a hair in the art of civilized warfare, and nothing in the book about unorthodox Indian tricks. By promotion of casualties, commander of a mob of juniper doughfoots on horseback, in a tight scrape where seasoned cavalry might well wish for howitzers. And, with it all, weighted with the terrific responsibility and drag of a slow-moving emigrant train.

Laish met the sergeant's eyes. He thought he caught in them a flicker of awakening hope. Probably a good man, this sergeant. Old soldier, most likely cursed with eastern garrison habits of orderly ritual, but capable within his limits. Not a leader. A reliable, steady noncom, whose strength had to come to him from his superiors, from an unquestioning confidence in their wisdom and judgment. He could hardly be blamed now if he was plagued by a sense of insecurity and a sick lack of faith. No doubt the whole command was infected by it. And the young lieutenant knew it, God help him.

"What else, King?" Laish inquired.

His use of the lieutenant's name, unadorned, was studiedly purposeful. It stemmed from his intention to establish immediately King's position, at the same time ringing a note of casual friendliness and informality. He firmly thrust from his mind the marvel of discovering how simple it was to assume authority.

"Fort Taylor was attacked without warning, four days

ago," King answered, as if dictating a report. He was all officer now, aiming very hard for a dispassionate detachment of tone and manner. "The hostiles charged right through, hitting officers' quarters first. All officers killed except myself. I was on O.G. duty, and I was able to rally the company and we drove them off. Attacks continued throughout the day, with increasing force as fresh bands of hostiles arrived . . ."

The position, he said, became untenable, which Laish could well believe. That night the lieutenant ordered the post destroyed, and he led the garrison in a break-out. The hostiles fortunately had failed to run off the horses. Two emigrant trains had joined forces and passed on west only the day before. The lieutenant conceived it as his duty, he said—with an involuntary glance at the brown-haired girl —to overtake the train and protect it.

"You've done well," Laish commented, and King showed a faint flush. The sergeant's strained mouth relaxed. The girl raised her face again. "What are their tactics?"

"Almost hourly raids all day long."

"Trying to wear you down, eh?"

King's lips spread in a grim little smile. "They *are* wearing us down, sir. Our casualties are heavy. The edge has gone out of the men. They're green to all this, and they can't take much more."

And then came the haggard, hated admission, compelled by biting honesty: "The command is falling to pieces, sir!"

Laish took his eyes off him. It was not pleasant to watch King's expression at that moment. He addressed the sergeant. "Is it that bad?"

The sergeant hesitated, hating like King to speak of it. The company was new and only half trained in arms. It had been given horses that not one in three could ride decently. But it was his outfit.

His weary eyes mutely pleaded, *What do you expect? God! Commanded by a brand new shavetail that they're not sure knows an Injun dog-soldier from a wagonhound!*

What he said aloud was: "They're slowing down, sir."

He meant, guessed Laish, that he was having to kick them up whenever the hostiles rode in on the whoop. A breakdown of morale was a hideous thing, contagious, a fatal disease that could shake the best of men. Laish had seen it in other men, in other circumstances.

King said, indicating the sergeant, "Sergeant Lybarger, sir. He deserves credit for duty performed under extremely difficult conditions. But I imagine, sir, you've come through a good many difficulties yourself, getting here." It was the closest he would allow himself to approach a direct question. He added something about his being sure that Mrs. Pepperis would be happy to know that the general was safe. An irrelevant type of remark, Laish thought it.

"Yes," Laish said, and he let it go at that. He watched the girl tie a neat knot and he quirked an eyebrow inquiringly at King.

The lieutenant cleared his throat. "Miss Christella Brunk—General Pepperis."

She finished knotting the bandage and closed the black leather case. As she rose, Laish bent forward and gave her his hand, helping her up onto her feet. His cupped fingers closed on her bare arm, and for a moment he held it while she stood facing him. Then he stepped back, doffed the campaign hat, and bowed to this girl, Christella. Some color washed into her face, while her clear eyes cooled. He held the hat low at his side, casually, and made his face blank and solemn.

They both murmured their acknowledgments to the introduction. Christella Brunk followed with a remark similar to that made by King—that the general's wife would be glad to know he was safe. She said it in a curious way, seeming to expect a response. Laish said again, "Yes," and after a straight look at him she picked up her leather case and left quickly.

When she was gone he turned to King. "She's surely not a doctor, is she?"

That look returned to King's eyes for an instant. "Her father was. She assisted him. Their train was held up at Fort Taylor for eighteen days with every kind of ailment including childbirth. Dr. Brunk worked himself to death on them. He took down with chills and fever and it went into pneumonia. God knows what she'll do in Oregon, alone."

"I doubt if she worries over that," Laish remarked. What he doubted was that a girl like that would stay alone long, anywhere she went. "She has her own wagon?"

"She has her father's wagon and team," King said. A pause, and he added in a carefully level tone, "At present she shares it with three critically wounded men."

Laish changed the subject. "How far to the Platte crossing?"

"Not more than four miles, I believe."

"Good. We cross tonight."

King gave a start of surprise. "Tonight? I'm told there are sandhills on the other side of the river. Perfect place for an Indian ambush in the dark. My own plan was to remain forted-in here tomorrow, to rest the men and the animals. And next morning send a strong scouting detail forward under Sergeant Lybarger to—"

"Lieutenant," Laish interrupted pleasantly, "I am taking command here, and I'm afraid I shall find it difficult to accustom myself to having my decisions argued over."

He spoke as much for the benefit of Sergeant Lybarger as for King. The sergeant needed strengthening. The whole command needed it desperately, by King's own admission. Lybarger would carry that strength to the men. The word would swiftly pass around that a jingo general, Pepper Andy, no less, had arrived and taken hold. It would at least stiffen the ranks, and give confidence in leadership a long boost. It would stave off that hideous risk of panic. Anything was better than that.

"However," he pursued, disregarding King's crimson face and stammered apologies, "I'll explain my reasons. It's common knowledge out here that the average Indian doesn't like fighting at night, if he can avoid it. If he's killed at night he wanders forever in darkness. Or so he believes. They may deal us mischief, some of them, but they're not likely to stage an ambush of any serious size, or a total attack. Not in the dark. Not unless they've changed their religion."

"I've heard of some such savage superstition," King acknowledged embarrassedly, "but I did not feel that it warranted—"

"It warrants our moving beyond those sandhills before morning," said Laish. "If we stayed here we'd get damn little rest tomorrow. These Indians are ripe. They'd chop at us till we made a run for it—and they'd catch us at the river-crossing in daylight. It's probably about what they've had in mind from the beginning."

He was speaking now from the experience of a gunfighter who had learned to estimate an enemy's points, good and bad, and predict his probable intentions. He could see little essential difference between one killer and an army of them. The tactics had to be much the same, the purpose being the same.

"And if you value Sergeant Lybarger," he said judiciously, "it would be wasteful to send him out. You'd never see him alive again, or his men. It would suit the Indian strategy of wearing down your command, chewing it off piecemeal—"

He broke off there, recalling that doomed buffalo bull hounded to death by the wolves. The analogy was fearfully apt: the emigrant train lumbering in hopeless flight, fleet wolves tearing at it and closing in. A chill rippled along his spine.

"There's a hired guide with the train, I suppose?" he asked.

"Yes, sir," King answered. "Two—Lurton and Croshaw. Lurton volunteered to go on to Fort Laramie for help, and he left the night before last. The help should reach us in eight days, cutting it fine. Croshaw is still with us."

"Sergeant, go and ask Croshaw to come here, please."

Sergeant Lybarger departed quickly, impatient to spread the news. Lieutenant King pulled himself together and asked if he could offer the general anything: food, whisky, cigars?

"Some whisky and a cigar, yes, thank you," Laish requested. "I'll eat a bite later on."

He was smoking one of the late Major Wycoff's cigars, the welcome tang of some excellent whisky on his palate, when hurried footsteps sounded lightly and a woman's voice called, "Andrew! I couldn't believe it when Christella came and told me you—!"

CHAPTER 4

THE SHOCK knotted his nerves and muscles up tight, and he sucked in a grunting breath. The cigar and the whisky glass dropped unnoticed. He glared in wild disbelief at the woman who came toward him in the firelight.

At first only puzzled, she slowed, paused, tilting her head slightly for a better view of his face in the faulty light of the fire and the lamp. Holding that posture, with her skirts lifted an inch by her finger tips, her figure in perfect balance above one small toe visible beneath the hem, she gave an extraordinary illusion of preparing a graceful curtsy to a dancing partner. Her rigors as an army wife, such as they were, had failed to rob her of that delicately enchanting quality, that instinctive charm, inherent in a Southern girl of breeding.

She came on another step, uncertainly. Recognition flashed, and her lips parted, but she uttered no sound. Laish saw the sweeping pallor, her eyes wide and staring in the mask of sudden whiteness. She drew her head back, raising a hand toward her throat as if fighting for breath, the wounded men watching her and King starting forward, afraid that she was about to faint.

"Mignon!" Laish said. He reached and caught her swiftly to him. She trembled like a small child too roughly captured by a grown-up, causing him to remember how she used to recoil instinctively from anything unexpected.

"Mignon!"—softer; a plea and a command. And the wounded men all eyes and ears, taking in the pretty marital drama, the reunion of the general and his young wife. And Lieutenant King clucking concernedly like a fidgety spinster reluctant to withdraw from the bridal chamber.

Laish rushed her abruptly out of the lighted enclosure, practically carrying her, brushing King back on his heels. She was as light as ever. He bore her, with long strides, around to the side opposite the shielded entrance. There in the dark, only some shadowy oxen looking on mildly, he steadied her on her feet and waited tensely.

He was shaken by a frenzied memory of other times, when she filled that too-brief span in his life, broken off behind him. The blindingly sharp picture blurred and dissolved. He crushed down his blood-pounding revolt against the civilized trivialities that forbade a man to carry off his woman forthwith, while inwardly damning himself for not having done so seven years ago. So he waited for her outburst and the torrent of questions, raking his mind how to meet all that.

It did not come as he expected. Gentleness and gay serenity were her ways. On the other hand, she was vulnerable to minor assaults of disturbance. As a little girl, she once told him, in games of chase and tag she was the one who pealed off shrill squeals when getting caught. They just popped out of her mouth and nothing she did could hold them in, she protested humorously.

It occurred to Laish now that he had never seen how she reacted to a major disturbance, all the time he knew her.

"Bart—it's you!"

Her voice, for all its breathless tremor, came softly to him, pitched low. Bearing the abrupt strain of emotion and amazement, it did not threaten to break. She was recovering control of herself.

"Really you! But how? Christella told me you were Andrew. You gave his name, and you're wearing— Bart, did you know I was here?"

"No," he said, "but I should have guessed, from what she and King said. I didn't think. Didn't realize it was your wagon train that got laid up at Fort Taylor and joined the Tillotson train. My thinking was all on something else. On myself, mostly. If I'd known—"

He gave a brief thought to it and discovered that there was little that he could or would have changed. By his own reckless actions in the past he had started the chain of circumstances, and each link afterward had presented an urgent contingency that he solved with the only possible expedient he could find at the time. The old saying occurred to him, that the ship that puts out in bad weather must be ready to trim sails and run with the storm.

He carefully framed a question and asked it: "Mignon— can you trust me? Wait! You must have heard some tales. Andy did. About me. Probably bad. And probably true, for the most part. When I tell you why I'm here, like this —I wonder if you will trust me then, or even forgive me?"

Her eyes glistened in the darkness, telling him that the tears had come. "Oh, my dear, when I think of what I did to you! Yes, I have heard. The bad things. The bad name. The black sheep. And I told myself, each time, 'That is what I did to him!' "

He didn't say so, but he couldn't help thinking that she took more than a fair measure of blame for herself. Personal feeling influenced her judgment, as it had influenced her husband when he charged all blame to the wild streak, thereby denying his own uneasy sense of sharing the responsibility. The truth lay somewhere between. Its precise location didn't much matter now, but privately Laish knew he wouldn't have explored the wild trail so thoroughly if he hadn't had some talent and taste for it to begin with.

He said slowly and clearly, leading up to the news that he had to break to her, "My mother's name was Pepperis, you know. I gave it as my name, to King and the sergeant. It is an honorable one, and Andrew added considerable fame to it, as a soldier. I resemble him only in appearance, and that only a little. He told me I look as old as he. An exaggeration, perhaps, but God knows it's not entirely false at present. I'm a bit surprised at your recognizing me so quickly."

"I knew you at once."

"So did Andrew, as soon as there was daylight enough for him to see me."

She asked swiftly, "You met him recently? Spoke with him?"

"Yes," he said. His hands still held her shoulders and he bent closer over her. "I wish I could have got to him a few hours earlier. His escort had been attacked without warning before sundown the previous evening. Yes, we spoke. But it was too late to—do much for him."

His preliminary words must have succeeded, giving her some forewarning by which she unconsciously braced herself to receive the finality. He drew her to him, her face pressed against his chest, listening to the choked little gasps and estimating the natural grief at somewhat less than heartbreak.

Stroking her dark hair, letting the sobbing go its course, he told himself it was a good thing for the heart not to stake heavily on anything or anybody. Nothing in life had permanence, and when the tearing loss came it hurt too damned much. He wouldn't want Mignon to be hurt so, and he was glad she had got over being in love with Andy, if she ever really had been—and he had doubts about that. An overwhelming infatuation, more like it. Not permanent. Swank major, ribbons on his chest, good family, private income: a godlike hero to the respectful cadets. Young girl, breathlessly awed, tremendously flattered. . . .

He broke thoughtlessly into the lessening sobs, saying almost harshly, "Something Andy asked me to tell you. He hoped Fort Laramie might work it out. For you and him, I mean."

She wiped her eyes with her hand and drew back a little from him. "It was hopeless. He must have known it, surely. A month after our wedding—less than that—we both knew it was a mistake. We would have divorced, but there was his career. The scandal. His pride. And mine. You were gone then, nobody knew where. Can you understand, Bart?"

He could understand very well. It had been as predictable as the outcome of a cold-decked poker deal. Infatuation followed by disillusion. Nature, too, occasionally stacked the deck.

"Well, it's past. Played and paid. Andy aged fast. So have I. But you are young, Mignon, and even more beautiful than ever."

He listened to the throbbing rumble of the Indian camps, to a patter of unshod hoofs, and thought of the riding bucks circling impatiently on watch around the great ring of silent wagons. Tomorrow. Definitely tomorrow, the grand attack on the double train; smash the ring and drive it on to the murderous pile-up at the Platte crossing. The eager bucks would relish that sport.

Heavily in stake, he was suddenly robbed of his cool detachment, and he said to her, "I am wearing his uniform and using his name. Don't expose me, Mignon—or do I ask too much?"

She shook her head. "Oh, no. You must have good reasons. I'm sure of that, Bart. You were always honest, always unselfish in your motives."

Rash, he thought, to measure a man by what he once had been. He kept the thought to himself. "Andy is needed here," he said. "King is young and without any experience of all this. It's far too much for him. Worse, the men know it. They have no confidence in him. They're demoralized. He knows the rules and he believes implicitly in them, of course, but by and large the rules don't fit. This is not civilized warfare."

"I have heard Andrew express his opinion of the worth of tactical training—'paper science,' he called it—in Indian fighting."

"Yes, Andy knew the game. It's a military classic how he outfought the Apaches. But he can't be here." Laish paused, and brought out a half-truth. "He sent me on ahead. I've taken command, in his name. It can't do any harm. It may do some good."

She sought his hands and found them. "You'll do everything you can, I know that. I must go now and tell everybody my—my husband is here, and that he will get us all through safely. That will help, won't it?"

He nodded. "That will help them, yes. You have your own wagon?"

"An Army wagon, and a soldier driving. Good night, Bart."

"Good night, Mignon."

He drew a long, deep breath after she was gone. In a minute he remembered sending Sergeant Lybarger for Croshaw, the hired guide. They should be waiting for him by now. He tugged the creases from his tunic, gave his hat brim a yank, touched the hilt of his sword, and straightened up. Brigadier General Pepperis, of Indian-fighting renown, was about to issue orders that would get the whole emigrant train and its escort through safely. He hoped.

Croshaw turned out to be a little man, of a frail appearance that was probably deceptive. He was one of those who did not fit the plainsman pattern of swaggering infallibility. He wore a shapeless cap tugged low over faded blue eyes that seemed to wander aimlessly and focus on nothing.

He gave Laish a limp handshake, and just stood there gazing idiotically down his pointed nose. Laish motioned to him and walked out of the enclosure. The guide followed obediently.

Like a stray pup, Laish thought; and this was the man on whose judgment and knowledge of the country perhaps depended the fate of the entire emigrant convoy and escort, a total of well over five hundred lives, counting the children.

The wagon-ringed corral was a black space mottled with the blacker blobs of animals. No sounds came from the men in the rifle pits outside of the hushed circle; the grip of fear was on them, as it was on everybody. In one of the ghostly pale-topped wagons a child awoke wailing, a shockingly commonplace sound against the outlandish drone of the distant Indian camps.

Croshaw, shambling along behind Laish, said sparely, "I been an army scout. I was with the cav'ry down at Palo Duro."

It seemed cheap boasting, until that name—Palo Duro—registered. Palo Duro was where Andy Pepperis had forced the Apaches to cry quits.

The point of a knife pricked Laish in the small of his

back. "What's your game—*General?*"

For a long moment Laish stood motionless, both his hands winged out. Carefully, then, he turned his head and met a glimmering stare. The little man was dangerous. He was not to be fooled with. The knife dug urgently, a wiry strength behind it ready to thrust it full in.

Laish murmured, "You're sharp, Croshaw!"

"So's my knife! Where's Andy Pepperis?"

"He got jumped. Escort wiped out. Rasakura's bunch. I took his place."

"Why?"

Irritation rose in Laish. He considered having to kill the guide, and how to go about it. "So I could put through his orders, for one thing. Take that damned skewer off my back, Croshaw, or I'll break your neck!"

The pressure of the blade did not lessen. "What was his orders?"

The little man was direct in his speech and in action. Laish trimmed his reply accordingly. "Abandon Fort Taylor and escort the emigrant train to Laramie."

"That's being done."

"It's being botched!" Laish snapped. "Whole outfit lying here spooked in the dark, and the Platte crossing only four miles off! Cross by daylight? King's green to this country. He doesn't know any better. He'll learn, if he lives! But what kind of a sun-struck fool are *you?*"

Croshaw lowered his arm slowly. He pulled back, holding the knife straight down, ready. It was a skinning-knife made from a file. Tempered steel, ground to a razor edge. "I told him. So did Tillotson. Maybe we didn't go at it right. The lieutenant's runnin' the show."

"He's running it to the book."

"That's true. It's the wrong book!"

"It's not my book."

"Nor mine. He ain't no Pepper Andy. But neither are you." Croshaw fell silent, staring at Laish. Presently he queried, "What's your book? What would you do if you *was* Pepper Andy?"

"Cross tonight," Laish told him. "Cross the Platte in the dark. Get the wagons onto high ground beyond, if there's any. Hold back a rearguard in the sandhills for a crack at Rasakura's mob when they come after us in the morning. Hand 'em a setback, and this outfit might last till help comes from Fort Laramie. Do you reckon your partner got through?"

"Lurton?" Croshaw shook his head. "No. He didn't get far. I found him off the trail early this morning—what was left of him. They catched him in a buffalo wallow. What they done to him looked more like 'Pache work than Pawnee, if you know what I mean. Wasn't much left to go by, though, on 'count o' wolves. Funny thing 'bout wolves. They crop up every time. They seem to know. Every day there's more of 'em, like the Injuns, gangin' up around this train, waitin' for the big kill."

"Croshaw, how scared are you?"

"More'n I like to be. But I ain't told nobody 'bout Lurton. It's bad 'nough with 'em. If they saw what I seen— ugh!"

They stared at each other. Laish said, "If this outfit stampedes, it's the finish. Those bucks out there—" He left the rest unspoken: the orgy of slaughter, seizing of captives, the looting and burning. "You've got a Green River trader as captain, I hear. Tillotson. How good is he?"

Croshaw made a throaty sound. "He's rattled worse'n any emigrant. His own crew is drinkin', an' he don't stop 'em. Hard bunch o' roustabouts, twice what he needs for his five wagons. They keep messin' 'round with the emigrant women. There's trouble there."

"We'll put a stop to that."

"King can't hold them sojers to line much longer. Ly-barger gives 'em orders with his hand on his belt-gun. If them Injuns knowed the shape we're in—"

"They know," Laish said. "It's fixed for tomorrow, I'd say. Pepper Andy figured it might come about here. At the sandhills or thereabouts. He sent me on. He expected me to do what I could. It didn't include arguing with a damned prairie scout! His wife trusts me. Why the hell shouldn't you?"

Croshaw made his knife disappear. He faced up to Laish, and his faded eyes were bright and squinty. "All right. Who you might be, I don't know, but I'll string with you—as long's we agree. If you go wrong on me, I'll sure get you. Let's roll this outfit!"

"We agree, then. It's just as well, for one of us."

They walked back into the firelit enclosure, and there they found King and Lybarger waiting with a civilian whom the lieutenant introduced to Laish as Tillotson, captain of the wagon train.

The Green River trader was a long-jawed man with wide eyes that met Laish's with almost piercing force. He was large, impressively deliberate in speech and manner, and the fear in him was obvious. Croshaw's opinion of Tillotson was a fairly accurate one.

Laish gave him a nod and spoke to King. "We're moving on, King, soon as possible. Pass word to the people of the convoy to team up and make ready, please. Wagons will travel three abreast, in close column."

So far, so good; but he was short on military idiom. He skimmed over that trouble by saying, "King, we must avoid a confusion of terms. I'm cavalry. You're infantry. And here we have mounted infantrymen whose horsemanship can't be expected to—"

"Sorriest bunch you ever saw, General!" Tillotson put in.

It earned the trader a glare from Sergeant Lybarger. A soldier could break his heart over his outfit, and still resent outside criticism of it, particularly from a civilian.

Letting that pass, Laish went on: "So suppose I just explain what I want, King, eh? I want a platoon of men on both flanks of the caravan convoy. About forty yards out, well spaced in single file. The main command will ride rearguard. Croshaw, of course, will be up front. The leading wagons—"

"The leading wagons are mine," Tillotson made interruption again. "I must have more protection up there, General! I'm carrying valuable merchandise!"

Laish turned on him slowly, in a chill wrath. "My concern is with the lives of all these people. They are of first importance. To hell with your gahdam merchandise, Mr. Tillotson!"

The trader blinked rapidly and paled. He raised a shaking finger at Laish.

"Do you realize who I am?" he bellowed. "I have powerful connections! I am Barclay E. Tillotson—*the* Barclay E. Tillotson, biggest trader on Green River! I am captain of this train and I demand—"

"You what?" Laish batted down the mighty man's finger and all but broke it. "You'll take orders, or you'll quit the pack and go it alone! Furthermore, you'll keep your drunken crew away from the women, do you hear?"—he was thinking of Mignon when he said that—"or I'll chain 'em to the tail-gates! And you too!"

Tillotson gaped. He swung his head toward King, from whom he had been receiving polite consideration. King gazed studiously up at the sky, vainly trying to hide his astonishment at such scandalous language from a general. It was all wrong. Army officers were supposed to mind their tempers and manners in dealing with civilians, under whatever provocation. To threaten an important trader could easily lead to peremptory recall and a court-martial.

Sergeant Lybarger, standing by, wore a look of rigidly restrained joy. Croshaw's eyes wandered. There were grins on the faces of the wounded men. Corporal Dunnington, the man who had been helping Christella Brunk, touched the bandages of his sightless right eye. He went through the motion of sighting a carbine from his left shoulder, and abruptly he marched out.

To the sergeant Laish said, "Lybarger, pick me fifty good men for the rearguard. The best riders. The best shooters. Be sure that every man has a rifle and eighty rounds. Have we got a trumpeter?"

"Yes, sir. But fifty good men—"

"You'll do the best you can, Sergeant. We all will. Gah-dammit, we got to!"

"Yes, *sir!*"

CHAPTER 5

THE LONG COLUMN OF WAGONS rumbled through the night, three abreast and close-hauled, drivers urging on their teams of sluggish oxen or swearing at stubborn mules. It was a troublesome struggle to keep them all compactly together. Among the emigrants was the usual high quota of individualists who saw no reason why they shouldn't pull out of line for one cause or another, or go forging ahead of slower neighbors. They wouldn't have been there, wouldn't have been pioneers setting out for a new country, if they hadn't been imbued with a strong sense of personal independence.

A man fell under his own wagon wheels and broke a leg and his family wanted the train halted while they attended to him. A woman screamed that her child was having fits, was dying, and the husband wildly cursed the Indians, the heartless and incompetent Army, and the promised land of Oregon. A wagon wheel threw its iron tire and collapsed . . .

No halt. By order of the general.

The Platte and the sandhills had to be crossed before morning if it meant abandoning broken-down wagons and even sacrificing a life or two. In severe discipline lay the only remedy for the canker of demoralization that had already eaten deeply into convoy and escort.

49

Laish rode up the column to the head, exchanged a few words with Croshaw, and rode back down the other side. He did this, he told himself, to get a grasp of it all in his mind, and also to make sure that his orders were being followed. Out on the flanks the two platoons of mounted soldiers rode spaced far apart, each in his lonely nightmare of watchfulness, listening to the pony flutter of Indian scouts and their querulous coyote calls. They, the outguards, were half certain that there would be an attack at any minute. They constantly edged in toward the wagons, trespassing upon the prescribed forty yards, and the corporals had to keep driving them out again.

Personal inspection was necessary. Laish paid it to every wagon that he passed. When he saw her, the girl, Christella, he privately granted that he had lied to himself, for he knew that Mignon in the army wagon would not be far behind. That was his real reason for his tour of inspection. He knew Christella immediately in the starlight.

He touched his hat, put his horse about to face alongside, and said, "Good evening. Or morning. It must be well past midnight now."

She was high on the seat, driving her own team of mules. Fine big mules and, he was sure, a good wagon if she had helped her father buy or build it. Seasoned lumber; tires put on with a bolt in each felloe; oversize hubs and axles with at least three-inch arms; heavy half-springs, iron braces forward and aft, the wagon-bed caulked as tight as a boat, and the stakes high so that the bed could be raised a foot or more from the bolsters when fording streams. The forward wheels were just about as high as the back wheels, and the bows of the wagon-top were fitted to staples on the main box. A cord passing through rings on the outer covering of the wagon tops and under the carriage nobs on the main box allowed the tops to be tightened, like the head of a drum. Christella Brunk knew about such things. She had the calm air of knowing.

She returned his greeting in a quiet, reserved voice, the tone betraying to him a stoic fatigue. "Has that child died?" she asked him. "I haven't heard anything more."

"I don't know."

"Do you care?" The tone was unchanged. "Couldn't we have stopped just for a little while, and let me do what I could?"

The muscles of his jaw tightened. "Yes, I care," he said. The rebuke hurt. "No, we can't stop. This train must cross the Platte before morning."

"Must? Because you have ordered it so, General Pepperis?"

"It's a matter of the greatest good for the greatest number."

"You make that sound very harsh, sir."

"It is harsh," he assented. "You may soon see how harsh it can be." He flicked his hatbrim, reined around, and rode on down to the rear.

Damn, damn! Why did women have to be like that? He was so riled up he forgot to look for the Army wagon, and he cantered past it without speaking to Mignon or even seeing her.

The dust-eating rearguard rode in ragged semblance of a column of fours, the horses better trained than their riders. The men were armed with single-shot Springfield rifles, left over from the war—another false economy—and there wasn't a saber in the lot.

Lieutenant King saluted Laish and mentioned sounds of increased activity on the part of the Indian scouts. The pony flutters were getting on King's nerves. The book didn't say what to do about enemy scouts who whisked past you in the night like ghosts, and laughed at you.

Laish nodded. "This move annoys them. It's not likely that the main force will come after us until morning, though. They know we can't outrun them. They'll have their scouts ahead to keep tab on us. I want you up forward, King. I'll take over here. Keep in touch with me. Better take a runner with you. Sergeant?"

"Here, sir." Lybarger urged his horse forward.

The picked fifty for the rearguard, Lybarger reported, rode behind under Corporal Dunnington. That left sixty-three men, not counting the flankers and the wounded. The platoons were all mixed up as a consequence.

Laish thought, and said, "Sergeant, think of it as two troops, cavalry style. My troop, under Dunnington, will supply a skirmishing screen and will stage delaying actions where possible. Your troop—meaning all the rest—will stay close to the convoy, ready to support the flankers against any attacks that may break through the screen. My troop is the screen. Is it clear to you? I think between us we can make it work. For a while, anyway."

It was clear to him, Lybarger replied woodenly. As to whether it would work or not he ventured no opinion. He had never seen it tried. His mind was grooved to infantry, which stood and fought, at least in theory; not to the mobile quality of cavalry. Fifty skirmishers seemed forlornly inadequate against hundreds of pony-Indians, warriors, the like of whose cunning ferocity and daring the world had rarely known.

The sergeant watched Laish drop back to the fifty-man troop behind, and he shook his head, knowing very well that it was Laish, not Corporal Dunnington, who would personally lead the chosen fifty. What the hell kind of a general was this?

And the men knew. Trumpeter Hoback growled, "Hey, Sarge, how's it feel to share jobs with a general?"

"Save yer lip fer blowin'," growled Sergeant Lybarger. "Drop out, you Connecticut nutmeg, and follow him. Yer place is anywhere he is from here on, and don't you forget it!"

It was a whisper right down the ranks. It had already reached the troop when Laish circled in alongside Corporal Dunnington. Because of his bandaged eye, the corporal had to turn his head fully to see him. The corporal had never been that close to a brigadier's star before and he saluted with such a hurried flourish that Laish's horse shied.

"Take it easy," Laish murmured. More loudly, for the benefit of the others, he repeated, "Take it easy!"

They needed steadying if soldiers ever did. And although they were raw, the Army had pressed them enough to its pattern so that the word and presence of a general amounted to heavenly guidance. Presently the nerve-wracked silence began giving way to muttered talk. A horse reared up for no known reason, causing a flurry around it and raising a laugh.

Listening to them, Laish searched the worth of this troop as a whole and made mental note of voices and names. They sounded like a more than usually diverse bunch, but that could have been a misleading first impression. In any unit of the standing Army, particularly these days, there could be found a proportion of odd numbers. They enlisted to escape what they could no longer bear: boredom, failure, enemies, disgrace, the law.

"Wisht I had a mule," grumbled the rider of the rearing horse. "I've rid a mule plenty times. You ever rid a mule, Carqueville?"

"No, Malone," responded the cultured voice of Private Carqueville. "Nor cared to. It has been said that the mule is unapproached in devilment, born old in crime, of disreputable paternity and incapable of posterity, with dexterity in aught save trickery and kicking, and no affection at all. I prefer the horse!"

"Such vonderfool vords!" mocked a middle-aged corporal named Herkenhoff. "Give some to Arab. 'No' and 'yes' is all the vords Arab knows. Eh, Arab?"

"Maybe," said the Arab, whose name was Askel or something like it. He and Carqueville were friends, Laish gathered, and the best riders in the troop. It was well to keep that in mind.

The convoy slowed to a crawl and soon afterward it came to a standstill. A sharp popping broke out up front, mingled with shouts. Like wildfire the alarm raced rearward from wagon to wagon: Indian ambush. Massacre. Who said they didn't fight at night?

The shouting and the crying fanned the blaze of panic, and Lieutenant King's runner tearing by didn't alleviate it. The runner drew up, to inform Laish that the foremost wagons were stalled at the Platte, under fire.

Laish rose in his stirrups and called, "Sergeant Lybarger! Ten men out to support the flankers and hold all wagons in line, by force if they have to!" And quietly to Corporal Dunnington, "All right, Corporal, let's see what we've got here."

It was a hell of a way to couch an order, but Dunnington understood the meaning: *Let's see what this bunch of ours is made of!* It prided the corporal enormously, the inference that his own worth was above any doubt. His crackling command rang with the authority of a regimental sergeant major.

"Right half wheel, double quick—march!" An infantry command. Laish was hitting up his horse, so Dunnington snapped, "Gallop!"

And up the halted convoy column thundered the doughfoot troop on horseback, headed by a bogus one-star general and a one-eyed corporal, not an experienced cavalryman in the lot.

As in any cross-section of humanity, among the emigrants were chronic grumblers and obstructionists whose endless complaints infected others around them. They cursed the general and his troop for having stayed at the rear, and from the vantage of hindsight they all claimed to have predicted an ambush.

Everything was confusion up front when the troop arrived. The head of the column had mushroomed and broken against the great sandy slough of the Platte, and stalled wagons stood facing in all directions. One had capsized in cramping the front wheels, and some men were working to extricate the driver while his wife screamed at them as though they were to blame. Meantime, spasmodic gunfire echoed across the river. An occasional bullet whistled overhead or smacked loudly into the timber of a wagon.

Out from the chaotic tangle stalked Tillotson, the Green River trader. He was followed by Lieutenant King. Croshaw cropped up beside Laish from somewhere, riding an undersized mare. Laish heard Christella Brunk's voice in the noisy darkness, inquiring if there were any injured.

Croshaw called mildly to Christella, "Nobody yet, 'cept that blame eediot under his wagon, an' a coupla Tillotson's mules."

Tillotson came up and, not seeing Laish among the troopers, in the darkness he bawled, "Time you tin soldiers got here! Damn that general and his flanks and rearguard! He'd let us all be—"

"Lieutenant!" Laish rapped. "Throw that man into one of his wagons! Tie him face down on his damned merchandise! And gag him! We'll have no sage-brush sailor insulting this man's Army!"

The trader cooled off fast. "I—I apologize!" he stammered. "I'm upset, you know, and excited. Hardly knew what I was saying. General, believe me, I'm terribly sorry!"

"You'll be sorrier if I hear your yawp again!" Laish promised. "Let him go, King, this time. What's over there, Croshaw, can you figure out?"

"Twenty or thirty, maybe," guessed the guide. "They don't see us, or they'd shoot better. They aim to hold us off till mornin', for the main bunch to come up and bottle us here. This crossin' ain't ever been easy, best o' times. The bank over there slopes up to the sandhills. Got to double up the teams. This," he mentioned, reminiscently, "is where the Fontenot train got wiped out in '63. Used to be you could gather bits of the wagons along the river. It made good firewood when it dried."

"Let's not renew the supply," said Laish. "King, pull some order into this Irish clambake, please, and have the column ready to cross in an hour. Or less. The sooner we move out of here, the better."

The better, he meant, for morale. Delay was a robber of courage. Activity was a potent stimulant.

"Corporal?"

"Sir?"

Here it was—the test of this troop in offensive action, not as part of a shaken company desperately fighting a defensive retreat. Laish met Corporal Dunnington's eye and could sense his uncertainty. There was no guarantee that the troop would hold together. Every man in it realized that Croshaw's guess of twenty or thirty Indian snipers might well be a rank underestimate.

A rousing talk would produce less encouragement than a bullying shout. There were times when words shrank to the trivial insignificance of a stale barracks joke. It was best to be casual and commonplace, thereby implanting the thought that the troop's readiness and ability were taken for granted.

Laish said, "We'll go over in skirmishing line. At the walk, till the trumpeter sounds off. Our purpose is to clear the way for the convoy."

He walked his horse down the bank and heard them come on after him, Dunnington riding to and fro to get the line formed out. Not one of them spoke a word, and Laish searched for something to say that might loosen them up. But he could think of nothing offhand that would not sound to them either too starched or ostentatiously fraternal, coming from a cavalry commander.

Then through the muffled crunching of hoofs in sand he heard the voice of Private Carqueville, singing in a clear tenor:

> *Return to thee, dear?—I would if I could—*
> *But I left my country for my country's good . . .*

The pseudo-sentimental quality of it loosened them and fetched up a satirical chuckle here and there. Corporal Herkenhoff carried it a bit further with the solemn comment that he vouldn't vonder if it vas so.

So the mood lifted, and when bullets began striking around them they had a margin of buoyancy to help them through. Malone's horse rolled over and sank under him in shallow water; Malone floundered clear and waded on in the wake of the rest, cursing at getting ducked, but voicing no sorrow over being rid of that unpredictable animal.

The river flowed in broad streaks divided by sandbars, nowhere deep enough to wet a stirrup. At one point the Indian gunfire ripped along a sandbar directly before the riders. They could see the spurts of sand, and the line wavered.

Laish said to the trumpeter behind him, "All right, sound off."

He had wanted to hold to a walk to within fifty yards or so of the far bank, but there wasn't time now. He looked back and wiped a glance from end to end of the advancing troop. It was still holding together rather well, considering the firing.

A man cut his hand upward in a protesting motion and toppled out of his saddle. Laish wondered which one, for he was already beginning to know these men as individuals. Malone, following in the rear, slogged toward the wounded man.

Trumpeter Hoback blared the sharp, rapid call, putting all he had into the final note, and the line swept forward with a great splashing and a roar. Corporal Herkenhoff bellowed something in German, and Carqueville laughed at him, and an ex-pugilist from New York shouted, "Skin 'em alive-o!" But mostly it was just a wordless, savage yelling.

Hoback went wild and sounded off again. It drowned partly the cry of another falling trooper: "Oh, God—I'm—"

They came out of the river like that and charged up the steep-sloped bank at the gun flashes spearing redly above them. The flashes dwindled and abruptly vanished. Laish looked behind to see the thin line coming strong, and he spurred his horse to a dead run.

Hard on his heels the troop topped the slope, beyond which dipped the first hollow in the folded sand hills. All the ridges, and the hollows and troughs between them, lay roughly parallel to the bend of the river, as if the sandy terrain had been squeezed back into great creases. This first crease was alive with darting figures, like vermin suddenly uncovered; some of them paused to shoot at the mounted invaders rearing up over the lip of the ridge, and then whirled and ran on.

A trooper went hurtling, his horse tripping and pitching end over end down the sharp incline. The line roared into the hollow and struck without a break in momentum. Laish, a jump ahead, was instantly in the thick of it, the troop rushing by and curving in on the fight.

In their scornful confidence that they could hold back the emigrant train until morning, the Indians had a cook-fire burning down in the bottom of the hollow. They had tethered their paint-daubed war ponies not far from it. Getting to their ponies ran them a high cost, that spot becoming the choice target. The wild-eyed animals threshed madly about, lunging away from their leaping masters. A die-hard knot of braves, cut off by Herkenhoff and a dozen troopers, fought like frenzied fiends till clubbed by the butts of empty Springfields.

The fighting degenerated to flight then, to pursuit, and here and there the swift slaughter of wounded tribesmen who would not give up. One, a bullet through his neck from Laish's pistol, flopped over on the ground and scuttled toward Laish with a lance raised for a straight cast. Carqueville raced across, a superb rider swinging his rifle by its muzzle like a polo mallet, and there was a smack. The Indian catapulted backward and crumpled.

The fast firing slackened, ceased, leaving an acrid fog of dust and burned powder in the hollow. Somewhere a fleeing Indian hurled back a raging scream.

Laish found Trumpeter Hoback and Croshaw close by him. He had not known until now that Croshaw had ridden over with the troop. He remembered to say to Hoback, "Sound the recall."

A glance around the hollow showed him that the way

was indeed cleared for the convoy. In far-off lodges there would be loud wailing of women when the tale of this night got back to them. Thinking of that, he felt an unreasonable depression suddenly clamp its weight on him. Although the squaws were said to be as merciless as the bucks, a crying woman was a terrible thing. He watched Croshaw drag a dead warrior to the fire, by the coarse black mane of hair. The returning troopers gathered loosely around.

He dismounted stiffly, handed his reins to Hoback, and walked in among the troopers, saying to them, "We did all right!"

Croshaw kicked the fire to a flare, and he looked down at the lean, limp body of the slain Indian. It had on high yellow moccasins and a dirty red headband, and in between was nakedness except for a breechclout. The contorted face had blue marks over the heavy cheekbones.

"Bloody thunder!" Croshaw breathed.

He raised his head and peered up at Laish, who asked sharply, "What's wrong now?"

The guide frowned, lowering his faded eyes as if embarrassed. " 'Paches," he muttered. "These was 'Paches!"

Laish caught Private Carqueville gazing strangely at him across the fire. It came to him then that he should recognize immediately an Apache when he saw one, and not have to be told. General Andrew Pepperis had made his reputation fighting the Apaches down in the Arizona and New Mexico territories.

He said to Croshaw, "You don't reckon they've come up to join Rasakura, do you? Aren't the Apaches hereditary enemies of the Pawnees and Shoshones?"

And that, he knew as soon as he said it, was also a blunder. There were bound to be bands of roving Apaches willing to make a temporary peace with old tribal enemies, in order to share in the loot and massacre of a wagon train. It could be that Rasakura had accepted their aid, though perhaps grudgingly. They were dreaded prowlers and born raiders. It was said that they had the stomach to fight even at night. There was nothing in their religion, such as it was, to deter them.

His blunder shook Laish out of his preoccupied mood, and he ran a rapid glance around at the faces visible in the firelight. He was vastly relieved to meet no stares of puzzlement or suspicion. The aftermath of violence gripped the troopers. Each had his thoughts turned inward upon himself and what he had done, and some of them were beginning to evince normal attacks of the shakes. It was entirely possible that they had missed what Croshaw said, too. They were so new to the West that the tribal difference between one fighting Indian and another made no great difference in their estimation.

All except Carqueville. That slender, thin-faced man kept watching him—like, Laish thought, a poker player who had spotted marked cards in a high-stakes game. Carqueville's expression had altered to one of intrigued interest and a strangely intense eagerness. It was as definite as speech, and Laish's next thought was: *He's caught onto me! He knows I'm a fake, and there is something he wants from me!*

Askel, the Arab, was close by Carqueville as usual, packing a tiny wad of tobacco into a little black pipe. Carqueville gave Askel the reins of his horse to hold, and he came on around the fire, drawing from his pocket a rare object— a clean white handkerchief, folded neatly. He pointed to Laish's left arm and said, "Allow me, sir."

Laish looked down at his arm and saw for the first time that the sleeve was slit and blood-soaked below the elbow. Where he had got that in the fight he didn't know.

He raised it slowly and let Carqueville tear the slit down to the cuff and lay the sleeve back, exposing the gash in his forearm. Carqueville shook out the handkerchief and refolded it to fit as a pad over the wound, and took off his yellow bandanna to use for a bandage. Weirdly, Laish got a whiff of perfume.

It reached his nostrils through the dominant smells of sweaty bodies, of clothes worn too long, and horses and rank Indian grease and acrid powdersmoke; and it made him think of Mignon, for the scent was jasmine, faint but unmistakable. He brought the pad of handkerchief up closer to his nose, the motion halting Carqueville, who waited with his bandanna and looked on watchfully.

His reactions, Laish knew, were being gauged and analyzed for a purpose. This was a deliberate test, to see how he would take it. The husband of Mignon could be expected to display a startled puzzlement, and jealous anger next; even the estranged husband, Pepperis. An impostor, unfamiliar with that perfume, would show nothing.

For it *was* jasmine: Mignon's perfume. And the handkerchief was Mignon's, small, of fine linen, having a rolled edge. Before the blood of his gashed forearm soaked through it, Laish made out clearly on the corner of the uppermost fold—folded for him to see it—the embroidered *M* initial.

His mind geared quickly to probabilities and possibilities, its promptness not at all clogged by emotion. There had passed those eighteen days at Fort Taylor when Mignon was held up there in the delayed emigrant train. And this man—this scapegrace gentleman-trooper, Carqueville —had been stationed there with the garrison.

It was possible. It was probable. A beautiful young lady, without love, the too-young wife of a veteran cavalry Indian-fighter who was everlastingly elsewhere. A cultured young man, a misfit who had no doubt made a wreck of his life, gently and respectfully adoring her, perhaps singing to her in that clear tenor voice of his on a moonlit night. The general's highborn lady and the trooper with a narrow bunk and thirteen dollars a month. . . .

It was not impossible. It had happened before. Young romance never did bow its neck to social distinctions. A terrible loneliness must have haunted Mignon these seven years; it could have led her into errors, this one not the first.

His face showed a reaction that in some way missed passing the test of Carqueville's critical inspection. An overly careful control of his features, perhaps. A gambler's blank mask donned too readily. He heard Carqueville say almost gaily, "Now I'll tie it, sir." But Carqueville's eyes said: *You are not her husband—you are not General Pepperis!*

The task was deftly executed. Having finished binding his yellow bandanna around the little white handkerchief, Carqueville stepped back.

"I think it will be all right, sir," he remarked pleasantly.

His eyes met Laish's once more while he saluted, but now they conveyed a sincere respect, and so did the meticulous salute. In the meaning behind his innocuous remark Laish could construe no malice, no taint of irony, but simply a guarded expression of faith. Carqueville approved and, like Croshaw, would keep silent as long as the imposture worked to the welfare of the wagon train.

"Thank you, Carqueville," Laish said. It was less hard than he would have supposed to match the man's sincerity, forgiving him the significance of the handkerchief, telltale keepsake. He had, himself, cherished a curl of Mignon's hair in a gold locket, like any man of sentiment. And lost it, he couldn't remember when, and God knew where.

"Corporal Dunnington!"

Dunnington did not answer. Outside the firelight a kneeling trooper called back in a muted voice, "This here's him, sir. He's—gone."

That was bad. Corporal Dunnington had been liked by all, and during the last hour he had displayed a valuable steadiness. He would be missed. Since the annihilation of officers in the dawn raid on Fort Taylor, sparing only King, noncom's stripes carried importance and authority. The men at the fire moved uneasily, every face turning toward Laish.

He kept his somber thoughts cloaked and stifled a sigh. There would be further losses, more gaps to patch up somehow. The death of individuals could not be allowed to crack the spirit and unity of this team of men.

He said to Herkenhoff, "Corporal, have the troop mount and fall in. Yes, in fours. We'll rejoin the column now."

Croshaw, frankly pessimistic, drew Laish aside out of hearing of the troopers. "This," he muttered, "is the worst fix I ever seen! I can't figure it out. Why, it's years on end since Pawnees kicked up any big trouble o' this kind! Oh, a bit o' robbery here an' there, a murder now an' then—sure! Nothin' serious. They didn't raise a hand against all the other wagon trains that went through this spring. What they got against this one? Hell, any other time they'd help us run these 'Pache skulkers clar out o' their territory, like they would a bunch o' Sioux!"

The question was not one that Laish could solve. It was true that the Pawnees long ago had agreed to keep open the trails running through their territory, and it was generally acknowledged that they honored the treaty. Their war was everlastingly against their Indian neighbors, particularly the arrogant and encroaching Sioux on the western boundary, which kept Pawnees out of mischief as far as white men were concerned. As army scouts and auxiliary warriors the Pawnees had no equal. They had helped the army smash Red Cloud, mighty Sioux war chief.

Laish felt less than qualified to analyze the wayward whims of any Indians, Pawnees or whatever. The cause of Rasakura's animosity was obscure to him, he informed Croshaw, but the effects were all too damned obvious. "He's out to get us, and that's a fact. To do it, he's willing to drop old grudges against his neighbors and recruit them against us."

Croshaw pulled at his nose, glaring squint-eyed at the dying fire. "Yeah. Shoshones, some Crows, Sacs—an' now 'Paches! God save us, what's got into the big cuss. What's he after? There's somethin' in this train—or some*body!* Injuns don't gang up that way. Not Pawnees, 'specially. Less'n there's—"

"A definite main objective. Yes. That's what Andy Pepperis said."

"He did, huh? Sure, he'd know that. I wish he was here! Somethin' wrong in this train. Wrong, I tell you!"

"The whole damned show is wrong," Laish said tiredly. "Knowing it and gabbing here about it doesn't help. Alright, I'm not Andy Pepperis, and for hell's sake quit reminding me! I'm doing the best I can!"

"I know that. I seen it." Croshaw let his nose alone and straightened up as if about to make the most important pronouncement of his whole life. "I didn't mean no offense to you," he said.

At the river, Laish said to Hoback, "Sound the Trot."

"Sir," gulped the trumpeter, "I don't know the cav'ry calls!"

"Sound any damned thing," Laish grumbled, "just so it's good and loud! Let the folks yonder know this man's outfit is coming back with its tail up!"

And so they forded back to the waiting column at a churning trot, with the trumpet pealing out beautiful flourishes of the General Salute.

It was a haywire outfit, for sure. It didn't even know the right calls.

CHAPTER 6

B Y CAJOLERY AND SOME MILITARY MAGIC Lieutenant King had succeeded in impressing a fair amount of order onto the head of the wagon column. He was still at it, his manner less correct and restrained than it previously had been.

Some of Laish's roughness had rubbed off on him, for he swore at a Tillotson mule-skinner who narrowly missed running his team into a crowd of women. The wagoners were double-teaming, raising an ungodly riot of noise and profanity, and some of the women were crying, and emigrant men stood around in undecided groups staring at the returning troop—the Pepper Troop, as it was already being called.

King hurried to Laish, to ask how the fight had gone. His tone contained a hint of dissatisfaction over being left out of it. He was that green, an Indian fight promised glory and romance.

Tillotson's nine big wagons of trading freight, King reported to Laish, were about ready to cross. But the emigrants were in a muddle. The emigrants were arguing about whose teams were to double-up on whose wagons. They wanted to elect a new captain of the train, right now. They wanted to know how large a force of hostile Indians lay waiting on the west side of the river. The emigrant who had let his wagon overturn on him was dead. The widow

wanted a coffin for him. The Reverend Yount, an emigrant, wanted to hold a funeral service with all the trim-
mings.

"King," Laish broke in, "let's get started before they
want a gunboat."

He bid for attention in the uproar, with a shout, and he
got it. "Tillotson, start your wagons over! You others—
bring all the ropes you've got! We'll haul your wagons
across with our horses. That's all. Hurry!"

He turned around to Corporal Herkenhoff. "Ride back
to Sergeant Lybarger in the rearguard. Tell him to give
you half his troop. Their horses are fresher than ours. You
understand what's wanted here? You tie onto these wagons, three or four at a time. You jerk 'em across the river,
fast. Not much time left till morning. Don't argue with
these people. Don't stop for anything. We get 'em across!"

He stepped off his horse and stood half leaning against
its warm and sweated hide, staring unseeingly down at the
ground, hardly conscious of King beside him and the men
of the troop relaxing in their saddles.

The burden of command began pressing on him. Because he ached all through with weariness, he could not
quite capture that sureness of himself that was so imperative. He reviewed in his mind what he had done and what
had yet to be done, and the one seemed inadequate, the
other overwhelming. This thing that he had taken hold of
was a hopeless impossibility. It needed a miracle.

Lieutenant King moved, murmured something. Laish
heard Christella saying in that quiet, firm voice of hers,
"It is high-handed! These are free people. They are not
your subjects! They are not required to obey the heart-
lessly inconsiderate orders of any Army commander!"

He swung his head and looked at her. She was speaking
directly to him.

She said, "A woman is crying over there. She is crying because her husband is dead. She wants him to be at least decently buried, in some kind of civilized way—a coffin. Can't you understand, General Pepperis?"

He could understand. The sobbing widow had no concern for anything, compared with her dread of burying her husband on the harsh and alien prairie, without a coffin, without the familiar and reassuring trappings of a proper funeral. To her that was unthinkable desecration. It was perfectly understandable.

And Christella there pleading and demanding, intimating that he was a callous military brute overstepping the limits of his authority because of an arrogant and personal whim. And Lieutenant King—so obviously in love with her, deeply in sympathy with any cause that she championed and accepting it as right—was probably willing to reject the certainty of its risk to the whole train. Good intentions, but stepping-stones to hell.

"It is impossible," Laish said to Christella. "Even if we had the necessary materials for a coffin, which we haven't—"

"We have!" she contradicted him. "I can spare a few planks from the bed of my wagon."

And ruin that good wagon, he thought. "No. You haven't the right to weaken your wagon and chance its shaking to pieces later. You are our medical department. In any case, we have no time to build coffins."

"Coffins?" she echoed. And swiftly the grim comprehension; the soft question: "Are there others?"

"Four. We have time only to bury them as they are. I'm sorry."

He motioned, and she made them out for the first time, being brought forward from the tail of the troop. Four bodies strapped across the saddles of four led horses, Corporal Dunnington's among them, arms and legs dangling at stirrup-length.

"The emigrant will be buried," Laish said, "as they will be buried. Rolled in a blanket. It's the best we can do. There are also some wounded in this troop, I'm afraid. Will you look after them, please? We have no surgeon, as you know. Thank you. We shall appreciate it."

He gave King the names of the dead, for the record. Afterward he spoke of the burial detail. And during the digging he leaned more heavily against his horse and dozed off and on, standing. He kept thinking of Christella, a stubborn girl, a pioneer girl bound for Oregon. She would surely not be alone, if she ever got there. Her kind was scarce.

They buried the dead with all the honors that could be allowed by short time and scarce materials, on the bank of the Platte, in the dark of night. Omitting the slow march and the black-draped colors and empty boots reversed on led horses, Pepper Troop stood to attention while Reverend Yount recited:

"The Lord is my shepherd; I shall not want . . ."

The Reverend Yount had to speak loudly to make himself heard above the clattering racket of the passing caravan. Some of the drivers, unaware of what was going on, continued cursing their teams in strong language.

As the wagons rolled up to the river's edge, mounted troopers tied onto them with ropes fastened to their saddles and dragged them and the teams willy-nilly on the run over to the far side of the Platte. It all added up to a wild hullaballoo of shouting soldiers, expostulating emigrant drivers, screaming women and children, plunging animals, and careening wagons.

"Yea, though I walk through the valley of the shadow

of death, I will fear no evil . . ."

Four soldiers. Names to be scratched off the paymaster's roll. Each record to contain, under Duty, the final notation: *Killed in Action.*

Somebody going idly through the files in the future would check the date and would wonder. That was a quiet year. That was the year when Red Cloud and his Sioux followers were hiding away off in the hills, licking the wounds they'd got from the army and the Pawnee scouts. Nothing much happened that year for the broad sweep of history to record.

And one emigrant, killed by accident, who certainly had never expected to find himself included in a military funeral on the Platte. His widow knelt crying. A few women murmured around her. They kept themselves well apart from the silent troopers standing to attention, especially from the cold-blooded commander who refused a decent coffin for a dead man.

". . . And I will dwell in the house of the Lord forever."

Clearing his throat, Reverend Yount would have launched into a personal recommendation and eulogy of the dead emigrant, for he came from the same Illinois town, he said, and reckoned he was fitted to speak of a fellow-townsman's undoubted virtues. But Laish motioned for Carqueville and Hoback to step up front.

The troop had no blanks, and ball ammunition was not to be wasted. Carqueville alone fired off the three shots, and Hoback did a fair job of blowing Taps. The women helped the kneeling widow to her feet and led her slowly away, crying, and Reverend Yount went morosely with them, ignoring Laish's word of thanks for the service. Laish told the troop to go give a hand on the wagon-crossing detail.

He failed to hear Mignon call to him once from the

army wagon grinding along in the passing column. Because her driver was a soldier, she had to check herself from calling out to Laish by his right name. Rather self-consciously, she called, "Andrew!"

It did not break through his heavy preoccupation. It was just a voice among many voices shouting in the noisy haste, and a name that carried no meaning to him at the moment.

The driver of the army wagon offered to pull out of line and run back to the general, but Mignon told him not to take that trouble. No trouble at all, he assured her, to which she replied a trifle sharply, "It doesn't matter. It is not important. Drive on, please."

At the riverbank she bent forward on the seat, hands tightly clasped, her eyes searching the plunging turmoil of mounted men. They swirled constantly about, and the night and their uniforms made them all look alike, yet when one rode in alongside the wagon, her eyes stilled. His face came up through the darkness, and he said, "It is a rough passage, Mrs. Pepperis. May I carry you over on my horse?"

"No," she answered quickly. "No, we—I will stay with the wagon, thank you." She watched him rein back, inclining his head slightly to meet his rising free hand in a graceful salute that was quite extraordinary in a juniper doughfoot on horseback.

After the wild race to the far bank, it became plain to the driver that it *had* been a rough passage for the general's wife. She was crying, very quietly, her face in her hands. Still, it surprised him to hear her murmur a Southern-accented, "Oh, damn! Ah could just *die!*"

Laish didn't know when Christella passed by in the column, high on the wagon box, driving on to the crossing. She had heard the three spaced shots and the solemn cadences of the trumpet. It was all over by the time she drove up abreast of the five fresh mounds of earth. In the dust and murk only one man remained there, his bared head bent musingly.

Christella's wagon moved on with the column. When the girl leaned out and looked back, the solitary figure still stood there. She had a sudden and vivid impression that General Pepperis stared down there into a secret pit, entirely his own, seeking in it some answer to monstrous problems.

Lieutenant King had not been notified of the fact that Pepper Troop's fight on the west bank of the Platte had uncovered the presence of Apaches, on top of perils already piled overwhelmingly high, and Laish didn't bring it up until the long caravan was crawling through the sandhills beyond the crossing where the fight took place.

Probably because, like the green troopers, he didn't discriminate particularly between one Indian tribe and another, King took the news stoically. Enemy reinforcements had been cropping up right along, and he supposed they would continue, this being Indian country. He mentioned that the outguards had not reported any sign of hostile activities this side of the river.

As far as hostility was concerned, Laish sensed a good deal of it in King. He could easily guess the cause of it. It arose from his clash with Christella and her reaction, her immediate surrender to his hard reasoning. Upon the grounds of that reaction a young man in love could build layers of brooding jealousy.

King may also have detected an unguarded note, Laish thought; some hint of conduct, a look, a certain inflection of voice, natural to any healthy male on the loose, but condemned in a supposedly married man whose wife traveled in the same train. Undoubtedly love did endow a damnable perceptiveness upon ordinarily thick-headed people.

"You seldom see Apaches," Laish said, "till they're ready to let you see them. What we did to that bunch will make the rest more cautious. They'll watch and wait. They're like white bad men—the minute you leave a chance open, they'll strike!"

His reference to white bad men was, he realized, one more revealing little slip. If he didn't watch out they would accumulate and betray him. The hazard lay in his necessity to tackle present problems with the tools of a different trade—the shifts and dodges of a gambler and gunfighter. He knew the ways of bad men, American and Mexican and the cast-offs of odd nationalities that could be found in any border town or mining camp uncombed by law. Human nature being a world-wide product, it could be reasoned that bad Indians ran pretty much to the same infernal pattern. Knowing the pattern, by and large, he reckoned he could predict the probabilities.

The trick was to use that knowledge without showing it. No military commander ever sized up the art of warfare in terms of cut-throat poker and the quick draw. Not until now, anyway, Laish reflected.

His statement, though, had an effect opposite to what he feared. In mentioning bad men he knew what he was talking about and it rang the right note of seasoned experience. It impressed Lieutenant King sufficiently so that he cast a sharp, stern look around into the concealing night.

"You think they may be actually watching us right now, sir?"

All personal feelings and sentiments were correctly buried under a soldierly professionalism. The standard aimed at was a matter-of-fact tone and an impassive countenance. The veterans attained it naturally. It was the young ones

74

who occasionally overshot the mark. Laish felt a little sorry for King. Some men grew fast, and some took a hell of a time about it.

"There isn't a doubt of it. You may see them somewhere ahead. When you do, you will attack at once. At once! Don't wait for them to hit you. Break up their plan. Hit first and hit hard!"

He gave further instructions with a crisp decisiveness that he did not wholly feel, laying out the order of march. King was to form an advance guard from the larger part of Lybarger's troop, and scout out widely ahead of the train proceeding through the Apache-haunted sandhills. The two flanking platoons would hold their positions, well spaced out in single file as before. Sergeant Lybarger and a squad would ride at instant readiness to give support at any point of the mile-long wagon train in the event of an Apache stab and a break-through. Pepper Troop would ride rearguard.

In that order the column would proceed until Croshaw located a defensible camp sight. After the night's march, a rest for the animals was imperative.

There were firearms in the train, and a good many of the emigrant men could probably shoot well, but he could not afford to count on them as an effective force. They had their hands full with their women and children, their teams and cherished possessions, and their nerves were raw. Few of them had any faith left in Tillotson as captain.

They were a mixed lot without a recognized leader to hold them together. And yet, as Christella said, they didn't have to take orders from an Army officer.

It was up to the escort to shepherd the unwieldy big emigrant convoy through these sandhills and beyond to safer ground where they could fort in for a stand, before daylight, before Rasakura's army of warriors came roaring in pursuit.

"Have I permission to make a comment, sir?" King asked properly, evidently retaining a sore recollection of an Irish manicure previously earned and received. "It is our rear that will catch all the brunt of it when the Pawnees come up behind us. Pepper Troop—beg pardon! Your rearguard troop of less than fifty men—tired men on tired horses—seems hardly adequate back there. We don't know how many Apaches there are in these hills in front of us, but we do know that the Pawnee force behind us numbers several hundred, perhaps a thousand."

"That is so," Laish agreed. "But it's the best we can do. Your force will also seem hardly adequate, King, if you run into any large bands of Apaches ahead!"

A good thing about King, he conceded, was that he didn't scare easily. But that, too, could be due to inexperience. Time would tell.

He went on: "Our two flanking platoons are pitifully small too, if it comes to that. We're damned well outnumbered all around, and we've got to spread ourselves thin. The Indians know it as well as we do, damn 'em. Rasakura has fitted his whole strategy to it. He has cut us off from all communication, Isolated us. Worn us down. His next step should be to close in on us. The final grand attack."

"This, then, is a planned campaign? A kind of organized nutcracker movement—by Indians?"

King's voice was strictly calm, and gravely incredulous. Indians were not supposed to be temperamentally capable of large strategy. The haughty Sioux and the fighting Cheyennes notoriously regarded war as a gory sport, with personal glory the chief incentive and to hell with strategy and discipline. The rating of a warrior depended upon the number of his coups, and nobody could tell him when he should fight. In the strength of their individual enterprise, the organized white men had discovered their weakness. And thus Red Cloud, that mighty Sioux warchief, lay in hiding, blaming his gods for his disastrous defeat.

For rigid organization the Plains Indian had nothing but contempt. So said the latest and best informed book, the West Point book.

It was not to be expected, Laish supposed, that a fresh West Pointer would take into account the possibility that Indians could learn a valuable lesson, given the opportunity. Pawnees were favored as army scouts and fighting auxiliaries. They were adaptable. Rasakura had served under Pepper Andy. They had picked up the secrets of the white man's strength. They knew the game.

"Yes. A nutcracker. That about hits it." The descriptive term drew Laish's mental picture of the situation into clearer focus and perspective.

Here was the mile of emigrant wagons toiling through these sandhills. Apaches hovering in front of it, watching eagerly for a chance to raid and cripple it, to bring it to a fatal halt. Rasakura behind, with his thousand warriors and his acquired wisdom, waiting only for morning to cross the Platte and smash the train, crunch it.

"The jaws of the nutcracker will start closing on us at daybreak, King. That's when the Pawnees will come on over the river after us. You must break through the Apache jaw at your end. We at the rear must hold off the Pawnee jaw. You understand, I'm sure."

There was no misunderstanding, no cloudiness in Lieutenant King's mental view. He made that plain with a nod and a minute's silence. With only the bare bones of his military training to refer to, and no flesh and muscle of experience, he could examine the anatomy of this calamity and recognize the stark desperation of Laish's maneuver. The whole purpose and business of the maneuver was to buy time for the wagon train, offering in payment the lives of the escort, the juniper troopers, more than likely the rearguard.

King did not see it as a risk, but as a fatal certainty, and with quiet fury twanging his tone he said, "It is an extreme resort, sir!"

Laish nodded. "The Apaches are extreme in their habits. Don't let them take you. Don't let them break through to the wagons."

That end of it was not what King meant. What filled him with helpless anger was the necessity of the sacrifice. For at this moment he knew and he shared the regard that the men of Pepper Troop felt for Laish, and he did not believe it very likely that he would see him alive again. He would have said something about it, but Laish reined off and cantered to the rear.

The sandhills, lying in a series of ridges, like waves and troughs, were bounded by the river on the east side and by the grassed prairie on the west side. Laish halted Pepper Troop and conferred with Corporal Herkenhoff.

The wagon train had got through, after a couple of brushes up front with darting Apache parties. It was emerging onto the prairie, and Pepper Troop had dropped back to stay in the sandhills.

"We'll dismount here," Laish told Herkenhoff. "We'll go back to the river on foot. Leave a few men here to hold our horses. Corporal, can you fix this spot in your mind so that you could get it straight? So you could get back to it in a hurry after daylight?"

Herkenhoff looked all around, methodically checking the dark contours of the surroundings. A sea of sand, tossed into billows by the action of steady winds, the billows twenty feet high, some higher. It was unlike anything seen in Germany.

"Yes, sir. I t'ink so."

"Make sure of it. Pass word to the others to do the same. From here on I want silence. We'll go back to the river in single file. You bring up the rear."

He led them through the sandhills, to the hollow where the fight with the Apaches had taken place, where the troop had met its test and come out well. They crept one by one into it after him, Corporal Herkenhoff last.

Signs of that fight remained, but not the paint-daubed slain. The Apaches must have slipped back and carried off their dead. It was queer to think of those lean brown shapes, startlingly alive, slithering silently into this hollow to drag slain brethren away to lonely burial trees. They had snaked in and snaked out, and Satan knew where they were now, far away or near at hand.

Laish climbed up the last ridge and peered out over the river crossing. The streaked Platte lay empty and soundless, but from the east and the south beyond the lower bank on the opposite side came a rumble of unshod pony hoofs on the march. The Pawnees were moving.

He slid back down into the hollow. He slapped sand from his hands, using the moment to make a final weighing of the task that he must call upon the men to do. This place was known to them. Here they had fought before and done well. They had that background of victory and the reminder of it. That was all to the good.

He motioned with both arms circlingly for them to gather around him. And then he gave it to them.

"We're here to hold off Rasakura's mob," he said. "Or stall them off. Do you get it?"

They were not sure. They simply looked at him, waiting,

trusting him.

He said, "We'll stick at it long enough to give our folks a chance to get through the hills and make fort on the prairie. This, what we're doing, is called a delaying action in the book. To hell with the book. The way we're going to play it, Mexicans call it the *'boscado.'* That means laying for the other guy just when he's dead sure he's got you stampeded. We're not stampeded. They only think we are. You get it now?"

Maybe they got it. It was hard to tell.

"Don't fire till I give the word," he said. "Don't fall back till I give the word. We're not going to stampede. Play it my way and we'll deal 'em the damndest hand they ever saw. We'll deal 'em hell!"

Out of the dark crowd of silent listeners came Carqueville's tranquil murmur: "Long live the *emboscadores!*"

"Right! And any trooper who gets killed," Laish promised, "I'll make him a corporal!"

That fetched a wryly appreciative chuckle. These men were finding toughness and a combative pride in themselves.

At a growled command from Corporal Herkenhoff— who, as Lieutenant King had done, forgetfully addressed them as the Pepper Troop in Laish's hearing—they deployed up the ridge. They stretched out in prone position overlooking the wide and shallow river bed. Some of them found scooped holes left by the Apache snipers. The troopers had no superstitious reluctance about making use of the holes, but there were a few whispered comments on the lingering smell of rancid grease and sour sweat.

Askel, the Arab, found a damp and hairy object that had been laid out to dry and left behind. The Apaches had evidently been raiding up from the south before making alliance with Rasakura's mixed horde. Murmuring in a strange tongue, Askel buried the scalp. He would not say whether the hair was short or long, black or fair.

"*Mek'toob*," he said softly to Carqueville, who nodded in somber comprehension.

The drumming grumble coming up east of the river droned steadily louder while dawn drained the blackness from the eastern sky. Sound and light advanced together in eerily fateful unity as though they were compounds of a single element, until the men on the ridge had imaginings of unearthly power rushing at them.

The Arab gazed east into the bleaching sky. Malone ducked his head and made a sign with his right hand. Other men fingered their triggers tentatively, haunted by the recurrent old worry that maybe this time the rifle wouldn't shoot, maybe would misfire. There were times when a dud cartridge could kill a man; it could cost the life of the shooter.

The sky gained a great bright stain, seen low on the horizon rim through stamped-up dust. Racing, the bright blue ceiling roofed swiftly overhead and reached the west, and the sound was a roaring.

Lying flat on the sandy ridge, Laish felt a trembling. Ground vibration; it had to be that. The pounding march of an army of savage horsemen. He looked along the line of prone men. Each man, he guessed, was telling himself the same thing. Ground vibration. It couldn't be the shakes. A man just couldn't dare get the shakes now.

Holding to that simultaneous onslaught, the sun burst above the horizon as the Indian riders thundered over the eastern bank of the Platte.

CHAPTER 7

THE WARRIORS, Pawnee and Shoshone and all the rest, rode adorned in all their masculine splendor of war paint and tossing plumes, lean-muscled bodies sharply etched into the blaze of dawn. The metal of their weapons flashed hard glints and the dust behind and around them was a yellow incandescence.

Laish caught his breath, shaken by the number of them and by their massive confidence. These were not far-roving raiders like the Apaches, motivated wholly by greed for plunder and lusts unleashed in transient victories. These were fighting men.

This was their land and the insane wrongness was the fact, repeatedly in evidence, that the land's vastness did not give room for them and for the white man to live in it without hatreds and slaughter. Somebody, red or white, committed an evil breach; the flimsy dikes of peace collapsed and war flooded the land. Somebody had done so again, and the tribes were up to pay off the score and to fire once more their old hope of driving the intruders out forever.

There could be no other answer to it but bloody resistance. There could not be for years to come until one side or the other lay too beaten to rise again.

Through the nerve-stretched moment of watching,

Laish gripped his pistol tightly, vaguely aware of a sudden gush of sweat drenching his forehead. He felt the wrongness, unreasoned like the premonition of death. There was the enemy, a tremendous force of fighting men advancing with victory already tasted. Over here waited his little troop, the impudent half-hundred, to dispute that grand advance.

The Indians gave an appearance of dancing their ponies at pause on the far bank. Laish stared hard, not sure. A wondering relief eased his strain, immediately followed by a deep stab of anxiety. Some animal sense, he concluded, must have warned them. They would now split and surround the troop. They would smother it out in short order and race on unhindered after the wagon train.

Hoback drew his trumpet closer to his face and exclaimed in a hushed voice, "Creestopher! Look at 'em come!"

The Indians had not paused. The bank over there slanted gently downward for some distance and kept them placed full in the sun, creating the illusion of suspended progress. Thickly massed, the Indians dropped down onto the riverbed and rode out over the crossing. They were coming head on. Nothing had warned them.

Their sound spread forward, two-toned, splashed water becoming audible in the heavier thumping of hoofs. Laish lowered his eyes to the advance, beneath the level of the rising sun. Daylight brightened swiftly and he could see the first riders moving on from one streak of water to the next. He was then detachedly calm and not at all tired, a familiar and dependable reaction rising to him from other days and other circumstances. He smeared the sweat over his face, and it felt cool and fresh on his skin.

Corporal Herkenhoff threw a hurried and instinctive look rearward. Laish noticed it and he said, "We may be a bit late for breakfast this morning, corporal."

The German flushed. He spat a squirt of tobacco juice off to the side with a strong attempt at nonchalance. It didn't do and he knew it, for an old canker was itching him and he never could mask his eyes. He was not a coward, no. He would bash in the head of anybody who called him a coward, like he did that Uhlan years ago.

Only it was that to crouch and to wait was not the same as to charge. It was that some men had horror of being caught; not killed, but captured. And these red devils . . .

"Ready to fire," Laish said to him conversationally, and Herkenhoff passed it along the line.

After this the Indians would split, if the fire-power was strong enough. They surely wouldn't charge on into it. "Heads down, and wait for the horn. Take your time."

Laish shook his head at Hoback, who was tensely thumbing the mouthpiece of his trumpet. "Wait!"

He watched the ripple of the Indian horde, rising on the trot over a sand bar, dipping into a slough, rising again. This had to be calculated and timed right. This must not misfire. To shoot too soon would be as bad as to wait too long. Short on firing practice, the troop as a whole was a bolo bunch, requiring each trooper to pick his man in his rifle sights at easy range for effective shooting.

On the other hand, there was the hazard of nerves breaking if drawn too taut. He heard the deep-throated talk of the tribesmen. Their leaders were that close.

Corporal Herkenhoff's length shortened on the ground, the knees drawing up uncontrollably. From that crucial sign Laish took his cue and he gave the order.

"Now, Hoback!"

Dry-lipped, Hoback burst breath into his trumpet and hit a clinker. He sharped a raucous shriek, got his tongue in it, and smeared it to a weirdly fluttering wail, but it served the purpose, and more.

The shocked Indians hauled in, staring, incredulous.

The volley ripped into them from the Springfields. It smashed the gaudy assurance. It plowed open gaps of struggling wreckage in the halted ranks, and there was instant consternation, Indians wheeling into the pack behind them and crying out. One of them came tearing on, a long-haired young buck staging his showy fling at reputation. He jolted off halfway up the ridge, his pony pitching headlong a jump farther.

The Springfields snicked on the reloads, setting up a dry rattle. A faint breeze drifted the smoke back into the troopers' faces and much of the next volley went for noise. The Indians split up.

It was then that they heard a distant crackle of gunfire behind them, west, from the direction of the wagon train. Lieutenant King's advance guard had run into trouble on the prairie beyond the sandhills, and was making a fight of it. He had found Apaches to attack, or they were attacking him.

Pepper Troop didn't hear the crackle for long, for the enemy before them raised an uproar. The Indians dashed about, their apparent confusion swiftly becoming converted into a recognizable formation—two outspread arms of horsemen reaching out widely to enclose the troop.

This was the split. Not a typical Plains Indian counter-move, done so promptly; a light cavalry maneuver, rather, such as would occur immediately to the mind of a man with army experience behind him. It was as though Pepper Andy were over there in command, himself, snapping orders, coldly shaping up the encirclement and annihilation of a hostile outpost.

The two long arms of racing horsemen curved around, one on the right, one on the left, at distant range as if to by-pass the Springfields. Fire-power, the sudden high toll of casualties, the stunning surprise of the ambush, combined to make the move logical. But a mob of unorganized warriors would not have done it without first indulging in a straight charge, each straining to outdo the others for the hell of it. The moves of the renegade army followed a deadly logic. They were predictable.

Laish called, "Fall back!" They had to get out of that pincer trap fast before it closed and caught them.

Once, in a rare spell of introspection, Laish had decided that every man has his lonely place and none speaks of it because it is a place of unspeakable fear and each believes his is the most shameful of all. The fear is gray and glaring and it creeps softly around that shunned place. But when at last the man must enter, and he knows that the door has closed on him, then fatalism, the calmness of the inevitable, rises to stand with him. He is then infinitely more dangerous, for a man who has stepped beyond fear is almost inhuman.

Pepper Troop fell back through the smoke-clouded hollow and abandoned it, and retreated over the next long hump in the sandhills. There wasn't a man in it who had not come to his lonely place.

They were on foot, separated from their horses by a mile of sandhills. This had to be an infantry action. They weren't there to skirmish, strike, and gallop off. Their job was to fight where they stood, retreat grudgingly, and keep contact with the enemy. Retard the enemy's advance, break his plans, make him work hard and long for this mile. The horses would have been an impossible encumbrance, useless except for flight, and there wasn't going to be any flight for Pepper Troop until the action was played through. The answer was footwork and all possible use made of the terrain.

Laish sang out, " 'Boscado!" And the troopers halted the short retreat, reversed, and flopped down behind the next sandy hump as if drilled to execute that outrageous order.

Even their cursing sounded preoccupied, inured by custom, no bite to it. All along the line the faces were rigid, beginning to set into the sardonic indifference of regulars who expected the worst. The Indians yonder outnumbered them twenty or more to one and were better armed for close fighting. They carried lances and short bows as well as their rifles. It wouldn't take them long to complete the two-armed encirclement, on their ponies. By the smoke of the Springfields they could mark exactly the location of that hollow, and surround it.

From this fresh position the troop would fire the next volley on the sound of his pistol, Laish notified Herkenhoff. Not before, no matter how close the Indians came. Complete silence until then, stay hidden and motionless, and if any man thought he had to cough he'd better choke himself.

"In a minute some of them will be right in front of us, I think—unless they spotted us getting out of that hollow."

No trumpet this time. Never pull the same trick twice in exactly the same manner, his training warned. Never fall into a predictable pattern of play. Let the other man make that mistake. The random move, senseless in itself, was invaluable as preparation for the unexpected. Deception, the finesse of good poker, required a margin of deliberate inconsistency. And gunfighting, too, was anything but the plain draw-and-shoot affair that the uninitiated believed it to be.

When the pony-riders slipped in from left and right, they came so quietly, not a sound out of any of them, that most of the hidden troop lay unaware of their nearness.

They had stretched and hooked inward the two enclosing arms, fingering ever so softly through the breaks in that corrugated washboard of sandhills, and now here they gathered.

They had gauged it beautifully to work swiftly in and make juncture directly back of that smoke-bannered hollow where the ambushing fire had ripped from, surrounding it and sealing it off. The absence of dust gave evidence that the soldiers had not pulled out on the gallop from that position. Therefore the soldiers must still be there, with their horses, waiting for the expected frontal attack.

Simple deduction. Logic. White men's logic. But the frontal attack and headlong charge was the costly style favored by the Sioux and Cheyennes and the like, crazy boneheads who lacked the sense gained from having served as army scouts under capable commanders such as General Pepperis. Pawnees were smart. In their every gesture and expression you could detect that consciousness of superior wisdom, the cocky bounce of the bright pupil challenging the teacher.

They trickled silently in, filling the wide furrow directly below and in front of the waiting troop. The light glistened along the smooth shafts and broad blades of feathered lances, and the breech-loading rifles bore a well-rubbed and oiled polish. Here and there a brown hand gripped a Crow tomahawk, a murderous invention constructed of a long knife bound crosswise to a horn handle.

And still Laish held his fire, letting the pot build up. At this distance, an easy stone's throw downhill, he was able to perceive that there were mostly young bucks. The main bulk of Rasakura's horde was holding back at the river, like a disciplined brigade at pause, waiting for its advance parties of young glory-hunters to cut off the enemy outpost.

They legged down off their ponies and, following an exchange of wordless signals all around, they swarmed on up the slope to overlook the hollow that they had so accurately marked.

Laish took aim with his pistol at a large Pawnee wearing a bearclaw necklace and eagle feathers and a cartridge-filled army bandoleer. The coarse sights of the center-fire .44 settled on a point between the shoulder blades and an inch or two below the base of the muscular neck. Shooting any kind of man in the back fractured the gunfighter's code of the fair shake. Contrarily, a leavening of saturnine comedy lightened it. Dead sure that they were catching the troop smack on its rear, spread out plain for slaughter in the hollow ahead, the grinning bucks were about to find the firecrackers tied to their own tails. Their backs were turned to the troop, and as they climbed higher up the slope ahead they ascended level into the rifle-sights of the prone troopers. Laish fired.

The big Pawnee leaped. He sprang up, his body poised tautly as if to dash on up the slope. Toppling backward, he screamed a word that sounded remarkably like profanity in English, which may well have been so. Most Pawnees had at one time or another had the opportunity to pick up some army blackmouth. They did learn fast.

The climbing bucks whipped around. Their scowling faces showed anger, actual indignation, not dismay. They contained such a sureness in themselves, such a reliance on their all-knowing sagacity, that they resented the shot as an unlooked-for affront, an insult. Then those of them who had climbed high enough up the slope were able to glimpse the poking round muzzles of the Springfields—behind them, not in front at all.

They were caught on the bare sandy slope, dead on the nail, as they had fully thought to catch the troop. Two hundred bullets could have riddled standing targets of regulation six-inch diameter at the short range, fired by bolo recruits.

The volley crashed out. It blasted ragged gaps, laid them jerking and rolling down the slope, sent the unhurt streaking to their ponies, the hastily mounted ones wrenching around to dash for cover and creating a chaotic tangle. The heavy smoke of the Springfields puffed and screened the rim of the hump, and the explosions of the cartridges joined to make a rattling echo of thunder over the sandhills and the river.

The sting of the smoke tingled and tortured the nostrils, but Carqueville called out, "Scrub your noses and shoot again!"

And Herkenhoff bellowed—"Shoot, *verdamt*—shoot!"

Shoot, damn it, Laish thought, *and remember the women back there in the train behind us.* His Colt roared. *Think of the women.* He thought of Mignon and Christella and then they hazed out.

"Fall back!"

On the barked command, Pepper Troop vacated through the gunsmoke of their own fire. Pepper Troop got out of there, on the run.

"'Boscado!"

Pepper Troop took up extended position five hills back. No casualties yet. The Indian losses running that high should soon blunt their fighting edge. So far, very good. Long minutes dragged by, the troopers lying in wait again, Laish tensely hoping that his calculations did not miss too disastrously the Indian reaction.

The furious bucks recovered their confidence. They staged a swamping assault up and around that hump. Too late. The hump was empty, and from their higher hill farther back the troop slashed gunfire at them as they bobbed up into sight. They split as before into two reaching, clawing arms, to gather in the elusive outpost of soldiers whose heavy shooting made any frontal attack too costly. They couldn't rid themselves of the conviction that the splitting maneuver was the smartest retort; it had always worked for the cavalry.

Again for Pepper Troop it was fall back, 'boscado, and they pulled the lethal Mexican trick once more. They got away with it, but with diminished returns. The wariness of the Indians ran about level to their rage; they were learning a new lesson. They crept cautiously and ducked fast.

Carqueville remarked pleasantly that doubtless the aborigines were harking to their native superstitions by now and wondering if these benighted sandhills perchance were haunted by the active spirits of heap-walk white soldiers, ghosts of the slain of the past days. It could likely be so. The Pawnees and Shoshones had never embraced Christianity with enthusiastic devoutness. They were Plains Indians, and in religious matters they differed stubbornly from the impressionable Navaho and Pueblo tribes farther west. They still liked their own wayward gods and mystic oracles.

Laish didn't want to play the trick again. Three times was stretching luck. A fourth attempt simply ran against reason. It defied principle and the laws of percentage and probability. A sucker bet, like the doubling-up system of roulette play for a player who possessed less than a million dollars with which to buck the tiger. He wanted to guard his few chips, hedge his betting. The chips were human lives.

Dammit, these were men he was gambling with: Carqueville, Herkenhoff, Hoback, Malone, and all the rest. He didn't want to lose them, not any of them. Two men already had bullet wounds from the last 'boscado.

But the troop's horses were still a good half mile in the rear, too far off to reach in a sprint through the clogging sand. Tiring legs and heavy boots were no match for fleet Indian ponies. Something had to be done to cover the troop's retreat, to save the men from massacre. He had a hope now of getting them out, having got this far, and so did they. One more slashing volley might discourage the hostiles for the rest of the day. It might raise doubts in their chiefs, even in Rasakura, that arch-renegade who thought he knew all the tricks of the army trade.

He had to play it.

"Fall back!"

" 'Boscado!"

It didn't work. Not that fourth and fatal time.

The Indians this time were a little slow in coming, and when they did it was on both flanks, creeping, with a feint at a frontal mounted advance for distraction. They had learned the trick. They had solved the strategem and they had struck upon the deadly simple answer to it.

It curled in silently, a stalking trap searching between the ridges. The bucks were playing it shrewd, out to pay off for the three times they had been hoodwinked. The main Indian force was growing impatient. Soon the massive scornful advance of Rasakura's brigade. For the young bucks of the two advancing arms, lost face, disgrace.

Conscious of a dark something near him, the last trooper on the left jerked his face to it and stared drop-jawed into glittering black eyes. He uttered a flat sound, between a grunt and a yell.

At the same moment the last trooper on the right loosed a wild shot. He too had looked full into black eyes of terrible hate.

Then the pattering stamp of moccasins, war whoops exploding like ecstatic shrieks of mad agony, glistening bodies leaping at the soldiers. The men at the extreme ends of the line disappeared into the writhing brown maws, and the line broke to pieces. Laish stumbled back to a fall with a bullet through his leg.

Corporal Herkenhoff ran to the right, calling, " 'Semble! 'Semble!"—until he, too, stumbled, dropping to his knees.

Malone swung over toward Herkenhoff, cursing him for a gahdam Fritz. A pony rider of the frontal attack came plunging over the sand ridge at them both.

To assemble was impossible. The swirling attack gave no time for a stand. Malone fired his Springfield at the down-plunging pony, the muzzle almost touching it. Laish saw the stroke of the rider's Crow tomahawk and its hideous impact on Malone's head. Herkenhoff, grappling the legs of an Indian who had seized his gun, shouted insanely again, " 'Semble!"

Laish brought down a feathered, yelling warrior with a shot from his pistol, and righted himself on one knee and made to push up. The troop was caught and swamped, fighting out of it. Two Indians streaking at him sprang apart to take him from both sides. The tribesmen wanted some living captives. It was insufficient that these soldiers should die quickly and only once.

Laish sank down and raised his gun. As he spent the cartridge, another gun exploded above his head. Then another. Both Indians dropped. Askel stepped around from behind him with his rifle smoking, and then Carqueville and Hoback on the other side. They were right there when he needed them.

They hoisted him up. He could stand on his left leg and maintain balance, but the right leg was numbed.

Blood was a warm stickiness in his boot. They rushed him along, rearward, and more men fell in with them to form a squad firing in retreat. Herkenhoff, hopelessly struggling in the Indian tide, screamed out in his nightmare horror while his captors beat and wrenched at him.

It was Carqueville who paused to level his rifle sights carefully and send a bullet cleanly into Herkenhoff's brain. Askel paused with him. Turning about, that task done, Carqueville looked at Askel, hearing the Arab cough, seeing the darkness spread all down his chest. Carqueville caught the slender body of the Arab as it lurched, and he carried it, hurrying on with the squad in flight.

From a rout it became a running fight, remnants of the troop converging in on the main group and sticking with it. The sandhills and the increasingly broken ground farther back made brief halts possible for reloading and for firing. Pepper Troop was on the run, trying to make its getaway. It should have been every man for himself, but they hung together, the best they could.

After their attack, the Indians abandoned all formation and whooped in mob pursuit. The main Indian force was moving up from the river. Their solid roar could be heard. The young bucks had to make good before their elders swept in and took the task out of their hands.

Near the last of the high ridges, not a quarter-mile from the prairie and the troop's held horses, Laish snapped his pistol empty and he swore. Less than a dozen Springfields were still firing, and not many more men than that were left unhurt. Several men, like himself, had to be helped; and some, like Askel, had to be carried.

They made one more stand in a hollow between sandhills. It was futile. Their fire-power was spent, no longer respected by the rabid young bucks, and a matter of contempt to the oncoming main brigade of warriors. Rasakura was advancing, doubtless angry at the unexpected delay and the hitch in his plans—as Pepper Andy, his teacher, would have been angry at the failure of his advance skirmishes to wipe out promptly an impudent enemy outpost.

"Fall back!"

They couldn't do it.

They lay like men stricken by fatal illness, and Laish looked at powder-blackened faces he seemed never to have seen before. Their gaping mouths rasped breath from throats dried raw. Bloodshot eyes glared a dull wildness. All features showed the slackness of inner collapse, except here and there among the wounded whose pain harshly forbade a letdown of sensibility. They were played out. Pepper Troop had shot its bolt.

"Hoback! Can you get to the horse-holders?"

His voice was a pinched croak. Until this stand he had not realized that he was in such a bad way. He watched Hoback push up, heaving, to a crouch. A bullet sprayed sand and struck something hard. Presently, fumbling, Hoback muttered, "Hit muh gahdam trumpet!"

A trooper lying on his back with a stomach wound suddenly let go and whimpered. Water was what he begged for, but it was more than water he wanted, much more. The awful sound of his voice said so.

Laish looked at him, his mind turning on what would happen after the Indians rushed in. They were getting very close, slithering over the broken foreground, and now the firing Springfields were reduced to seven. Seven men had managed to conserve some ammunition, or they had salvaged it from the dead and the wounded. And those rifles would foul up in another shot or two. No time to clean the black-powder scum from the breech blocks.

He thought: *Is this my doing? All these men?*

An impartial fairness answered, *No. We served our purpose.*

It couldn't be done without sacrificing a part for the whole.

I've made a better soldier than you dreamed, Andy. I figured the deal right. We held them back. Now we pay for it!

The rush of hoofs burst in at the time the firing Springfields were down to four.

Hard behind the loose horses of the troop, clumsily herded by the horse-holding detail, rode Lieutenant King and Sergeant Lybarger with most of the main command. They crowded the position, and in spite of the pressure of the moment they stared aghast at the wreck of Pepper Troop—the beaten and the exhausted. The bloody ones. The dead.

It was that, and he hardly knew why, that fetched Laish groping up onto his feet, to try to stand. He believed later that it was a kind of angry pride. Later still he recognized it as something different. What fetched him up now was Lieutenant King's failure at first to know him, and then exclaiming, "My God, sir!" in that tone of awed compassion.

He resented it, swiftly and fiercely, taking not at all into account his appearance that had brought it forth—not seeing himself as a haggard, burning-eyed scarecrow. He resented the young West Pointer at that minute, utterly disliked him, and he snarled at him, "Dismount your men and do some shooting, quick—this isn't any gahdam barracks parade!"

The lieutenant took it well, only asking rapidly, "A squad to help with the wounded, sir?" He reached to steady Laish on his feet.

Laish pushed the arm away. "We'll damn well get our own wounded out! You hit those hell-cursed stinking howlers yonder and cover for us, do you hear?"

Partly it was reaction from incessant violent strain. It flared up out of a white-hot rage at the hideous wrongness that resulted in all this. The collapsed faces. The dead. Men staring in sluggish shock at broken edges of their own bones. Carqueville, openly sobbing, holding the lifeless body of the Arab ever so gently.

"You horse-holders, steady with those animals!"

Gods of wrath roast those that caused the like of this, and kiss my foot the bunking lot of you gods if you don't.

"Lift the wounded on and stay with them!"

Would King never fire?

"Ah, Hoback, there you are! Good man!"

Leading up Laish's horse himself, Hoback helped him into the saddle and, mounting his own, reined alongside. Lieutenant King, he said, had just arrived with Sergeant Lybarger's troop when he got to the horse detail. The wagon train was forted-in clear of the sandhills, manned by armed emigrants, and the outguards were cracking off at some distant Apache riders who had been beaten off.

That was all Hoback had learned. It was evident that his estimate of Lieutenant King had risen considerably. "He wants us out, sir, before he volleys off," he mentioned. "Don't want to shake the horses, with the damage on 'em."

"Very considerate of him," Laish grunted skeptically. "Hope the Indians favor it! We will withdraw!"

The troop pulled out of the mess, no sooner out of it than the first crash of gunfire from King's relief reverberated through the hills. After that, the shrieks rising in the fading echoes. The Indians were catching it, their main force pounding up in clear sight and getting it slam in the face. Fire-power, fresh and strong. Another surprise for Rasakura, damn him. *Thought you had us whipped, did you? Hell—Pepper Andy didn't teach you everything. Andy never was much of a hand at the poker table. And he didn't know a whole lot about how Mexican outlaws fight on the run.*

The second, third, and fourth volleys boomed smartly at even intervals like a minute gun inflexibly timing the progress of Pepper Troop straggling forth to level ground west of the sandhills. The drooping soldiers straightened a little in their saddles, thinking, like Laish, of the morning's final and climactic surprise that the Indians were getting.

It wasn't likely that Rasakura would muster his force for the grand attack on the wagon train today. Not this day. It wasn't a bit likely.

Pepper Troop had bought a day.

CHAPTER 8

THE WAGON TRAIN lay corralled on a rise of ground on the prairie shaped like a blunt arrowhead, reached by shallow slopes from the sandhills on the east. West, the shoulders of the campsite fell away sharply and were toothed with shelf rock, forming a natural barrier to mounted attack.

It was the best campsite for the purpose, Croshaw declared, this side of Fort Laramie. It was defensible, and it overlooked the surrounding terrain. All it lacked was water.

Having eased off the cavalry boot, Christella sheared off the blood-caked leg of Laish's breeches and exposed the knee. Her hands were facile and sure, but Laish noticed their slight tremble of fatigue, and he raised his eyes again to her face. There were blue shadows under her eyes.

She had organized a women's squad from among the emigrants, to tear bandages and help care for the wounded. But the brunt of it all fell on her, for she was the only one in the train with actual medical knowledge.

"How many disabled?" he asked her. He would get a straight report from her, no half-truths. He knew that.

He lay on the ground, on a canvas wagon-sheet, half of

which was propped up with spare axle-trees to shade him from the blazing sun. This was his command post, with the flag planted out front and a runner sprawled asleep where Laish had told him to get some rest. The whole camp was like this, quiet, too weary to pay attention to the occasional shots of the outguards.

"Today? Twenty-three wounded, nine seriously." Christella examined closely the hole through his knee. "Missed the patella and came out on the right of the tendons, but it isn't clean."

"And eleven killed," he said. "God, that's hard."

"Yes," she murmured. "Today I learned how hard it can really be—the greatest good for the greatest number."

She was kneeling on the wagon sheet, and she raised her head and met his eyes. "For what I said to you I'm sorry and ashamed. I ask you to forgive me."

Suddenly she was all angry flame, utterly at variance with the quiet self-possession that he had come to associate with her in his mind. Her breasts rose tightly in her dress, and color washed high on her cheeks, while her lips pressed bloodless. "This morning I wished I were a man! I wished I could be there fighting like a man!"

She was a furious comrade, hating the enemy. Hating it fiercely and whole-heartedly for what it had done, and for what it would do. "Why do you smile?" she demanded. "Are you laughing at me? I'm not one of your silly delicate creatures! Haven't you ever known a woman like me?"

A smile had started on his worn and dirty face. It vanished as he spoke: "No!"—as sharply as the slam of a door.

Acute embarrassment heightened her flush. "I'm sorry. I shouldn't have—"

And she didn't finish that, for she was thinking, of course, of Mignon, her friend and the general's wife. Not by a word would she intentionally be disloyal to her friend.

Mignon had gone deathly white at sight of the blood, and she had to be bustled off to the army wagon. It was a hell of a way for an army wife to react, but she couldn't help it, couldn't be blamed for it; the general had always meticulously ensconced her in some comfortable billet surrounded with gracious culture, and never before had she been within a hundred miles of a battlefield. Mignon belonged with the sheltered and the dainty ones.

"Don't be sorry," Laish said, and now he smiled fully for her. "Please don't. I was smiling at what you said, because I was thinking of all that you have done and are doing. It wouldn't do for you to be a man, Christella. It wouldn't do at all."

She bent quickly over his knee again. Her skirts, stretched taut by her kneeling, spread their hems in the dust. She tugged absently and impatiently at them. "I'm afraid some cloth from your breeches went in—it looks like a cut-nosed bullet, from the wound. Cleaning it out may hurt. I'll have to use a probe."

"The trick," he said, "is to concentrate thought on something else. All thought." He kept his eyes on her. "Even pain can be outwitted, up to a point. I learned that trick years ago. It's a good one, when it works."

"Up to a point, yes," she agreed. "But not the pain of others. That's a hard trick. Doctors should know it. They don't, sometimes. So sometimes they wish they weren't doctors. My father never did learn it, God rest him."

From the forted-in ring of emigrant wagons she had been witness to a sight that she would never forget: Pepper Troop's crippled return.

A ragged procession of poor riders, worn-out men holding up the wounded, and the wounded helping one another. Limp bodies, arms dangling down one side of a horse, legs down the other, and riderless horses following nervously in the rear. They had come plodding up the shallow slopes, and Christella ran down to meet and help them, against the order to stay within the wagon corral, and women and men of the emigrant train streamed out after her. The hot tears. The broken troop.

Hoback, the incorrigible windjammer, pretending to mistake Laish's cough for a command. Sounding off General Salute on his bullet-punctured trumpet and cracking up in the middle of it. Men having to be lifted down, moaning curses, crying out when touched at the wrong places. That was the troop that had splashed back across the Platte flaunting such cocky pride.

After them from the sandhills soon rode Sergeant Lybarger's troop, Lieutenant King a rather dashing figure at their head. King's relief force had handed the Indians a beautiful lacing. They had done well, kept their heads. They knew their worth now. They rode with style, with a soldierly arrogance as high as that of Pepper Troop when it recrossed the Platte—and it was too terribly easy to foresee their future: when they, too, would come stumbling back from a sacrifice paid in the name of a delaying action to buy the emigrant train another day of grace from massacre.

It was then that Christella shook with fury at the insensate hostility of the Indians, and wished that she could go out like a man and fight and kill them. She knew that everything in her life, previous to this, was nothing more than a preparation. She was a pioneer woman; she knew that she could hold up her end.

Laish mopped sweat from his face with his filthy yellow bandanna, watching Christella bind up his knee after cleansing the wound. "Your father," he observed to her, "must have taught you well. No sons?"

"One," she answered. "He went bad. He turned to gambling. Then worse. Yes, my father taught me a great deal. Not only his trade. He threw away a safe and good practice to come West. He would be needed, he said, in the new country. He believed—"

She paused, smiling at Laish's abstracted stare at her hands, knowing he wasn't really listening to her. "What are you thinking of, General?"

He blinked. He brought his eyes to focus on her face. "I'm thinking of this wagon train. This double train. The whole outfit. All of us."

"Yes. I know."

"We can't stay here," he said. "For one thing, the water won't last. The horses. Teams. The people. Takes a lot of water. Tomorrow the Indians will be back on the attack. We're fairly safe here, but only for today. This is only a respite."

"Yes," she said again. "I know."

"We bought this day at a high cost. It was that, or lose all." He shoved his wounded leg out straight, unthinking, and winced. "Eleven killed. Twenty-three wounded. God! We can't go through that again. My troop is down the spout. They were damned good men. There was Askel, as good a man as you ever could find—"

He stared so intently into her face that she grew self-conscious, until she realized that he was not quite seeing her and was talking half to himself.

"And yet," he said, "we've *got* to go through it again. We've got to do it every day. Until we reach Fort Laramie. That's a long way. God, it's too far."

She asked, trying to relieve him, "Couldn't we hold out here until help comes? Croshaw's partner—Lurton—went to Fort Laramie."

He shook his head. "They caught him," he said absently, and was hardly aware of the swift catch in her breath. "No. We must keep moving on. This is a day-to-day thing. Each day gained means that much more to the good, as long as we're moving toward Laramie. We've got to gain every day. Buy it. Trick for it. That's the way it is."

He fell silent, beating his brains for a solution. He pulled up his ripped sleeve obediently when Christella said she would next clean and dress the gash in his forearm. The flimsy little linen handkerchief that Carqueville had bound it with had become a wadded lump. Christella had to soak the dried blood and dirt from the cut to get at it.

She did it quietly, not breaking into Laish's thoughts, and while she was so engaged Lieutenant King and Croshaw showed up at the crude canvas-hung command post.

King saluted Laish respectfully. He brought up the matter of Private Carqueville. Private Carqueville was insisting that Private Askel be buried as a Sunnite and an Islam believer. The Reverend Yount was sternly holding out for Christianity as the only proper service for a soldier of the United States Army, the army of a Christian nation.

Laish considered the problem and gave his verdict. "Let each hold burial service in turn, King. Private Carqueville first. He knew Askel best. He was Askel's friend. If Reverend Yount objects, you will please remind him that he's a civilian without authority in our *Army* concerns. We will bury our dead according to *their* religion, no matter what our own may be. That is an order. Convey to Private Carqueville, please, my sincere respects."

Christella rose, not yet finished in her binding of Laish's arm, and said to King, "I'll go with you, Joyce. It may be best"—she put the question to Laish—"if I set it to Reverend Yount as a tactful suggestion, don't you think so?"

Her unaffected use of Lieutenant King's first name did not escape Laish's notice. He nodded slowly, and watched them leave together. They made a handsome couple, even in the desperate and dirty extremes of this jackpot.

Laish felt old again, as old as he'd felt in the capsized ambulance way back with Andy Pepperis. And he looked it, he knew, although he was not yet thirty.

It occurred to him that Lieutenant King showed no green uncertainty now. King had the appearance and the manner of a crisply capable young officer. He seemed, like the troopers, to have picked up quite a high valuation of his own worth. He had beaten off Apache forays. He had got the emigrant train to a defensive position. He had turned around and rescued Pepper Troop. The men didn't spit behind Lieutenant King's back. Even Sergeant Lybarger was developing an almost amiable scowl toward him.

It was a good thing, Laish mused. Confidence in an officer was absolutely essential in this desperate scrape. The hazard of casualties contained a likelihood of King's finding himself in sole command again. He would be able to do better with the men than he had done before.

Laish saw King take Christella's arm, in a most natural way, crossing the wagon corral, as if owning the privilege to guide and protect her. That was too damned much of a good thing. Who the hell did that shavetail think he was?

The incorrigible male urge raised that question, Laish supposed, and he broke off his aroused gaze. The old Adam. He was a male animal on the loose, stirred up by the nearness of a desirable female, bristling at the presumption of another male.

It supplied the answer, until memory countered with a query about Mignon and Carqueville—a definite case of male presumption if there ever was one; yet he could overlook it. He could respect Carqueville without any qualifying resentment, and bring to Mignon a fond and gentle tolerance for whatever indiscretions she might have committed.

The inconsistent lapse disturbed him. He mulled it over, and solved it with the explanation that he had carried his love for Mignon around with him so long now it was invulnerable. All the jealousy was burned out of it.

Croshaw had brought shells for Laish's pistol, from the army ammunition wagon salvaged from the Fort Taylor disaster by Lieutenant King. He cleaned and loaded the Colt .44 for Laish, while discussing the wagon train's position. Prospects, he allowed, looked awful scrubby.

"I see them 'Paches an' them Pawnees an' all, visitin' back an' forth, like gophers 'fore a storm. I make it they're augurin' up mischief. Bad medicine! Both them parties, 'Paches an' Pawnees, has got to make good right quick. You *sabe*? 'Specially the Pawnees. I mean, after how Rasakura got fooled today. You know."

Laish nodded. He knew. Prodding beside their original main motive, whatever it was, there was now the additional spur of Indian pride. The bursting ego of the gunman, the bad man, the killer. In the presence of their ancient tribal foes, Rasakura and his warriors had lost much face this morning. They must regain it at any cost. The Apaches, themselves beaten off, would strain to outdo them and jeer at them. Prestige.

He pondered on it. Result, a contest in reckless daring. Apaches competing against Pawnees and Shoshones and Crows, for glory and pride. The wagon train, bone of contention; the hounded bull buffalo staggering to its finish.

His mind refused the vision and took an oblique tack,

and he found himself thinking of Askel, the Arab. "Even a dead man!" he muttered. "Carqueville and Yount—wrangling over his body. Cooking up their own little holy war! It's like a fire you can't put out. Rivalry. It flares up anywhere, any time, and anybody can get burned by it. There'll always be fighting, I reckon, as long as there's anything left to fight about."

And himself, he thought wryly, and young King. He and King were not exempt from the everlasting vice of antagonism, even now with all these human lives practically in their hands and dependent on their unerring judgment. They were men, mutually biased in prejudice—because Christella was a woman. To that extent, at least, they were wrong-headed and fallible and as unreliable as stallions snorting and whistling with the spring fret in them.

"We're all fools, Croshaw," he said.

The guide hadn't much of a turn for philosophic self-criticism. Struggle was normal to him. He had to live, and he graded as fools those who proved too slow in a scrape. To live anywhere—plains, forest, mountains, the Southwest land of little rain—meant sharp struggle. It meant reading the weather, knowing the ways of animals, outwitting starvation, thirst, blizzards, heat, trading with capricious savages and fighting them to the last rock when they broke out on the warpath. He squatted there on the canvas sheet beside Laish, gazing down his nose, twisting his tongue for words to express what he wished to say.

Being what he was, a good deal Indian in his settled habits, he preferred unfolding his opinions and sentiments gradually over a long period. It took time, that was the trouble, and time now ran short on an uncertain path.

Laish saw that something burdened Croshaw's tongue.

Any plainsman and mountain man lapsed easily into a white Indian, but rarely mastered the art of making a couple of grunts carry a comprehensive explanation. Laish spoke of the day-to-day exigency, the imperative *must* of pushing on westward toward Fort Laramie, the problem of beating off Rasakura's hostiles. "And yet not run our own strength down the drain," he finished. "God knows it's drained off bad enough!"

Croshaw kept nodding his head, stopping when Laish stopped talking. At the end of a long silence he cleared his throat raspingly and said, "It's a right job this far." That didn't cover it, nowhere near, so he had to come right out and say, "You're doin' damn good, Gen'ral."

Not sure whether the title sprang from an ironic reminder or not, Laish looked hard at him. "There's no need to call me that when nobody's around," he remarked. "I'm not any general, nor even a shavetail if it comes to that, and you know it. Would you be trying to whittle on me?"

Croshaw shrugged. "You're an awful techy cuss," he retorted, rising, and now he was more at his ease and he grinned faintly. "Gen'ral or not, it's you's runnin' the show, so what's the diff'rence? Pepper Andy couldn'ta done no better'n you done today. Not as good, maybe. His juice dried out down in them Arizona rocks. Your star's bogus, but your juice—"

He broke off. Two hands were straightening a loose sag in the upraised section of the wagon-sheet, their owner on the other side. The task done, a shadow passed along the sunlit canvas wall and became Christella, stepping on around the end of it into the shelter. She lowered her eyes to the surgical kit, which she had left beside Laish. It was only too obvious that she had heard some of the talk.

The two men looked on as she picked up the kit and

the bowl of water, not a word spoken. Turning to leave at once, she noticed that she had only partly completed the bandaging of Laish's forearm. She came back again, knelt, and put down the kit and bowl, still without speaking.

Over her head, to Croshaw, Laish said, "You've got a big mouth, for a little man!"

Croshaw thinned his lips, intolerably insulted, and his faded eyes froze. For once he had said too much, and it galled him to get hooked up on it. He had made a rare effort to deliver a compliment and the thing had backfired into a betrayal, yet he couldn't stand there and argue the injustice of being called a bigmouth. He sent Laish a glare of anger and stalked out of the flimsy, makeshift, canvas command post. The C.O.'s orderly slumbered on, the C.O.'s flag flapped lazily in a stray gust of dusty wind, and the C.O. racked his brains wondering what the hell to say to Christella.

CHAPTER 9

CHRISTELLA'S EXPRESSION OF FORCED COMPOSURE stayed unchanged when Laish said to her quietly, "All right— you overheard us. You know."

There was an almost imperceptible nod. That was all. She kept her eyes on what she was doing. The bandage went on evenly and firmly, spaced spirals overlapping an economical half-width. Bandages were scarce.

He said, "I'd better tell you all about it. Talk to you about it. Yes."

The "Yes" confirmed his own decision—the Pepperis habit. Odd that he should have picked that up, he thought detachedly. So like Andy.

Unintentionally, his voice hardened. "General Pepperis is dead. Been dead some time. About eight days, or nine. I've lost count. Rasakura jumped him, on the way to Fort Taylor. I took his place. I took it for good reasons which —uh—have since become pressing obligations. Unavoidable. Croshaw knows. He approves. And Mignon, of course. Carqueville has guessed it. He also approves. What is *your* verdict, Christella?"

For an instant she raised her eyes gravely to his. Lowering them to the bandage unwinding in her hands, she asked, "Who are you?"

This grew difficult, fast. His name was not unknown,

back in the trail towns and mining camps. A certain no-
toriety had become attached to it. Successful gamblers and
gunfighters attained that doubtful and risky pinnacle, if
they lived that long. Some mathematical-minded repre-
sentative of an Eastern insurance company had worked it
out that the occupational hazards of a professional gambler ran ten-to-three against continued health, and the
life expectancy of a known gunfighter covered slightly
less than four years if he stuck with his avocation. Seven
years strained the law of average. It made you prominent.

"My name," he answered her slowly, "is Laish. Bart
Laish." Confession, said to be good for the soul, he had
never found good for much of anything but a prompt
sentence—with escape a complicated matter of bribery
and hard work. "Andrew Pepperis was my cousin. Like
him, I was slated for an army career. But I—well, the term
often used is 'went bad.' I went bad."

He watched for a softening in her face, and he saw it
come. That brother of hers that she had mentioned, who
had gone bad. That eased the way. Probably a gambler.

"I became a gambler," he said.

What else to reveal? What temperate words could cover
all the rest of it?

"I drifted into a wild kind of life."

That was no lie. Just an understatement. Even in a law
court under sworn oath, a man wasn't required to incrim-
inate himself with detailed accounts of his misdoings.

"I enlisted to get away from it," he said. Was it necessary to describe to her the circumstances of the getaway?
He thought not. "In the Army, unfortunately, my past
caught up with me."

Such talents as his could not long lie dimmed. They
shone forth, particularly bright the last big poker game
on paynight, and also during the ensuing riot.

"It became impossible for me to stay in the Army," he said.

The guardhouse captain had believed he had made it quite possible, with a cell and a frigid promise to blast Laish's head off if he tried any funny business.

"So I broke—uh—I left the Army. I decided to make a fresh start in a new country where nobody would know me."

They gambled in Oregon as elsewhere, he presumed.

Christella tore and tied the ends of the bandage neatly. She rose from her knees and stood gazing out across the wagon corral. Her clear eyes, lost in a soft and womanly musing, held no condemnation of any kind, only an honest searching for decision.

At last she murmured, "It doesn't really matter who you are. Nor what you've been. It's what you are now. It's what you're doing. That's what matters. After what has happened—what you've done—I couldn't lose faith in you."

That got him, hit him like a child's expression of trust given in return for glibly false promises. He slumped back on the dusty canvas and said to Christella, "Don't have faith in me. You'll lose it."

She brought her clear gaze to him, waiting, unsurprised, and at that he let go the last frayed threads of deception.

"I'm a lying cheat, Christella. I'm a cardshark and I'm what's known as a gunslinger. Perhaps I wouldn't have been, though I wouldn't swear to it—but I loved Mignon, and she married Andy Pepperis, and I couldn't hang around after that."

His words came out unthought and unshaped by any careful construction; he had to tell her the blunt truth of it.

"I wouldn't swear to it, because I liked the wild life—

maybe would've taken to it anyway, on any excuse. Wild oats. Call it that. I loved Mignon and hated Andy Pepperis. An excuse. I went bad and liked it. When I enlisted as a trooper, it was to get away from the law—it was catching up with me. I deserted in a few weeks—broke out of the guardhouse. Shot a bucko captain. Spilled a few others. I'm on the long dodge. Civil and military—both want me."

He shielded his eyes with his bandaged forearm. "I've loved Mignon all this time," he said. "I think that's the only thing I can claim to have been reliable about."

Christella nodded slowly. Her eyes mirrored painful knowledge. She, too, had camped at Fort Taylor for eighteen days with the delayed train, and she was Mignon's friend. She had perception, an instinctive understanding, tolerant and humanly sympathetic, receptive to Mignon's confessions those nights when Mignon needed to speak of herself intimately, woman to woman. In years she was younger than Mignon, but Mignon never reckoned the count of years when whispering her secrets to a kindly ear. The discarded lover, long regretted. The unhappy marriage. Carqueville. Being Mignon's friend, Christella knew all about her past and her present.

She could never betray the whispered confidences. All she could say was: "Mignon spoke of you to me. I didn't know you were the one, until you told me your name just now. By your own admission you're a cheat and a liar, and worse. I think very likely you're a rascal. A bad man."

He brought his arm down off his eyes, to stare at her, struck hard by the simple truth of her statement, wondering at her intentions.

And then, leaving the shelter, she said, "I think I understand. I have faith in you. I believe in you."

"Thank you, Christella!" he called after her.

But she was gone, hurriedly, carrying her dead father's

surgical kit and the kitchen bowl of pinkish, dirty, antiseptic-smelling water. She was the medical department, and the commander wasn't the only wounded man in need of her attention.

A trumpet sounded Taps. After Mahomet and Christ, the army was putting in its lick of ceremony over the burial of one Private Askel, or name something like it, a soldier of the United States; Killed in Duty.

Laish kept thinking of Christella until, shaking his head impatiently, he picked up again the dominant problem hovering like a thousand madmen's daggers above the emigrant train. His eyeballs smarted, seeming to be embedded in a dry and gritty substance, and he closed their lids while trying tiredly to recall some trick that might be adapted and sharpened for use against Rasakura.

He awoke to the sound of a voice, Lieutenant King's voice, and he demanded drearily, "What the hell is wrong now? If it's Reverend Yount shouting the gospel again—"

"It is not, sir. It's the Tillotson crew." King's tone was strict with the effort of holding in his anger. "Same behavior as before—and worse. Drinking. Fighting with the emigrant men. Annoying the women. They are a disruptive element."

"Disruptive, yes," Laish conceded. He surveyed the young officer irritably. "But it's hardly the business of the Army to settle quarrels between emigrants and drunken roustabouts, is it? I suggest, King, that any emigrant who hasn't got the stomach to protect his own women from insult should have left them at home—should have stayed home himself, in fact! We have other functions to occupy us. The Indians out there are also a disruptive element."

King swallowed, and said, "Granted, sir! But—"

"In short, King, we will mind our own business!"

"Yes, sir. I am striving to do so." King's face flamed red. "It was my belief that—"

"And if you haven't enough to take up your time, then help the men clean their rifles, or something equally useful!"

"Very well, sir. But it was my belief," King got out rapidly, "that you regarded Christella—Miss Brunk—as our medical department. Under—uh—Army protection, therefore, semi-officially. Chr—hem—Miss Brunk has also suffered from insult, from Kardell, Tillotson's crew boss. I ask your permission to—"

"That we will attend to!" and Laish heaved himself up. He slapped on his dusty black hat and limped out of the command post. "We will personally scorch the gahdam ar off 'em!"

"That is what I had in mind, sir," said King, falling into step with parade-ground precision. He held himself ready and willing, and he didn't run short of courage at all; but it occurred to Laish that military correctness of procedure could be carried beyond reasonable limits. Had he been King, and wanted to give somebody a working-over, he damned sure wouldn't have stopped to ask permission.

Wouldn't have thought of it, for one thing.

The big freight wagons of the Green River trading outfit stood drawn up in a half-circle of their own, as if independent of the main emigrant caravan, forming a campsite that was partly private and exclusive. Unlike the common white-tops—painted invariably blue-and-red—Tillotson's wagons were dark green, with black wheels, and the boarded sides towered high, tops covered by tarpaulins lashed securely into place against rain and wind. They

were built to carry enormous loads of merchandise, and
each required spans of from fourteen to twenty mules and
sometimes more, depending on the grades and the state
of the trail.

They stood out monstrously, dwarfing the emigrant
white-tops, and by comparison they looked tight and ship
shape; no clattering washtubs and iron kettles strung on
behind; no dogs and pets, family cows, sunbonneted
women, children. An Indian-trading outfit, all men. A
tough outfit, so it looked to be at a glance, and so it should
have been. Hard-bitten and capable, pursuing business
and immense profits.

Traders, on the whole, helped to open up the country,
broke trail for later comers, and earned what fortune
they made.

Some didn't.

In this semi-private space walled by the huge green
freight wagons loafed the Tillotson outfit, an oversize
crew of fifteen men. Although they all bristled with re-
volvers and knives and good repeating rifles, there was no
attempt here to maintain guard as the emigrants and
troopers were doing night and day. A few of them dozed
in the shade underneath the wagons, by their abandoned
attitudes evidently drunk. Most of them squatted around
a spread blanket on the ground, with cards, and with piles
of cartridges serving as chips.

Poker, Laish noted; that new innovation from St. Louis
by way of New Orleans, called stud. With round-the-cor-
ner straights, most likely: Queen, King, Ace, Deuce, Trey,
so forth. First card holed, the rest showing, and your hole
card became the stinger if it filled the sequence, if there
showed any sequence. Essentially simple, containing ten
thousand complications. Pretty good game. Wild cards
complicated it further, but a gambler who trusted his

fingers and his wits could make allowance for that hazard.

"Aside from a little ordinary hell-raising," Tillotson declared, "my men haven't misbehaved."

His long jaw trembled slightly. "My God, General, what d'you expect? My freighters aren't Yount's psalm-singing schoolma'ams!"

"Nor we ain't monkey-sojers!" jeered his wagon boss Kardell from under a wagon, and the men eyed Laish with drunken insolence.

That was it. These trader's men regarded themselves as a privileged set. They were in the wagon train, but not of it; they were exempt from its chores and duties and common responsibilities. A hard-case lot, overbearing because able so far to bully the emigrant men, who were not a violently inclined bunch but just a crowd of movers heading West to free land which they would farm and make productive.

Tillotson sent Kardell a glance of uneasy warning. Laish caught it, and he said to Lieutenant King for them all to hear, "This gang seems to have got out of hand. It's about time to rope them out and bring in a squad to take over here!"

"You can't—" Tillotson began. He changed it hurriedly to: "You won't do that, I hope, General Pepperis! I—I ask you for patience. My men are all right. Thoroughly trustworthy, believe me. Tired, yes, of course. And—and discouraged."

So it was that too. And that posed an odd thing. For the emigrants still hung a finger-hold on hope. So did the troopers. They still believed there was a chance. They were not licked yet.

These Tillotson men, well armed, tough, experienced, were not betting on the chance. Therefore the drinking. Therefore Tillotson's loss of control over them. Demoralization did not always rot the softest spot first. The women of the train—by Almighty God!—were holding up fine. No panic there yet. No hopelessness. Yet these seasoned ruffians . . .

There had to be an answer. "How much whisky are you freighting with you, Tillotson?"

"Just a few jugs. No more than we need for ourselves." Tillotson caught the stare of his wagon boss, Kardell. He said firmly, "General Pepperis, you don't have the authority to take it! I will appeal to the whole train! Most of the emigrants have their jugs, too. You don't dare search every wagon!"

That was true. Laish watched Kardell tilt a demijohn deliberately and take a swallow from it. Kardell, he guessed, was drunk enough to make trouble.

He changed tack and said, "There'd better not be any more meddling with the women."

Tillotson took it as a sign of retreat. He shrugged. "Very well. But I swear somebody has been exaggerating the case to you. You know how it is. A man has a drink or two. A woman flutters her petticoats at him. Leans over and gives him a glimpse—"

King smacked Tillotson with his open hand, full on the mouth. Then he said formally to Laish, "I beg your pardon, sir!"—while Tillotson fell flat on his back in the dirt.

"Yes, King, of course," Laish murmured. He paid King small credit for it; would have paid more had King swung a healthy crumpler straight to the jaw. A slap did nobody any good, including the slapper. Hit hard or save it for the pay-off.

Tillotson sprang to his feet, replacing his beaver hat, slapping dust from his frock coat. Bitter strain bulged his wide eyes, yet he hardly spent a glance on King. He brought his stare and impressive deliberateness up squarely to Laish. His dignity topped that of a bishop rising from contact with a tripwire, fastening blame on the parent of the clownish child. At the spread blanket the men reared up, scowling, the well-worn cards forgotten in their hands.

Kardell came lunging out of the shade, to stand bull-belligerent, thick arms dangling, his eyes shuttling between Laish and King.

A bad bunch, Laish thought. A bad set-up. Frontier scamps, heavily armed, hating all forms of law and order. Nerves all raw from constant drinking, and from the squeezing clutch of Rasakura, which the drinking failed at last to drive away from the most sodden consciousness. King's small act of violence, slapping their employer Tillotson, merely concentrated their blind hatred upon a small facet of the forces threatening them.

Still strange and unexplained was the fact that these men, so much wiser than the emigrants in Indian motives and purposes, should at heart so despair of Indian withdrawal from attack. They saw no escape from it. The drinking stood as a symptom, not the cause of that sorry state; they knew something that others, the emigrants and the soldiers, did not know. They would not tell; they were afraid to tell. Something there was in this caravan that the Indians wanted, and these men knew it.

"Yes!" Laish said aloud, startling himself. It sounded so like Andy Pepperis. "How much whisky did you say, Tillotson?"

"A few jugs," Tillotson repeated. "A few gallons for our own use. You can't confiscate a civilian's personal property—I say it again, and be damned to you! Try it! Start searching the wagons! You'll have a mutiny on your hands, I warrant that!"

Laish agreed, privately. The emigrants would be bound to construe it as a high-handed act and a direct threat aimed at their own rights; and these were a fractious lot of movers, suspicious and resentful of anything that smacked of trespass upon their independence. It was hard enough to make them keep their wagons in line. Search one wagon, and you kicked a hornets' nest. They disliked Tillotson and all his tough crew, but they shared the same rights, and always there smoldered that old jealousy between soldiers and civilians.

Many of the emigrant men were drifting up to the Tillotson camp, to watch and listen, to keep check, to play umpire, with leanings toward the civilians and sharp eyes out for Army fouls. It was up to the soldiers to pull whizzing miracles, but they better not step on anybody's toes while doing it.

Tillotson saw that he had scored a point, a big one, and he dug it in. "There are limits, General Pepperis, to your command! These emigrants are not soldiers, praise be! As I hear you were told by Miss Brunk—they are not your obedient subjects!" Softly, for the gathering emigrants not to hear, he added, "You can't afford to antagonize this whole train!"

"That is the truth," Laish said, distinctly enough to be heard within a radius of fifty yards. "Nobody's trying to confiscate personal property, nor abuse the right of privacy —except the Indians! I'll buy your whisky, out of my own pocket."

He watched for Tillotson's reaction, but it was Kardel who blurted out scornfully, "You ain't got pocket enough, yallerlegs!"

Laish felt absently in a pocket of his torn and frayed breeches, and asked King, "Do you have any money?"

King, too, searched a pocket. "I—uh—have about fifty

dollars, I think. And a bank draft for—"

"We have enough between us, then," Laish said; and to Tillotson: "What's the price?"

Again the response came from Kardell. "To you—hundred dollars a gallon! Cash! None o' them bank drafts an' Army vouchers, an' sech!"

Laish raised his brows at the fantastic price. Still speaking to Tillotson, he asked, "Does your crew boss do your selling for you?"

"No," said Tillotson. "But the whisky belongs to him and the crew, not to me." He cleared his throat, glancing off at the emigrants. "I don't drink."

"You're remarkable," Laish complimented him solemnly. He ran his eyes over the crew. "So you all chipped in for the drinking supply. Kardell did your buying, I suppose. Does he talk for you, too?"

One of them sang out, "He sure does!" He was a thin and twitchy man, lying under the wagon that Kardell had vacated. He cradled a rifle in his hands, its muzzle resting between wheel-spokes. None of the crew disputed his statement.

Kardell said, "Got it straight now, yallerlegs? These is my boys. I talk for 'em, yeah! You bid to buy our whisky. All right, I set the price. That's fair an' square, ain't it?" He chuckled, winking largely around at the crew and then at the emigrants. "I doubt you an' the shavetail's got the price of a jug—but there she is. We'll sell you all we got at a hundred a gallon. Hell, we aim to 'commodate a star yallerlegs like you, any time!"

Laish nodded. The listening emigrants, he reckoned, were rather enjoying the Army's dilemma. Everybody liked seeing tall authority laid back on its ear. He could relish the like of it himself; it was so damned ornery and human.

"That is fair," he said. "We've got it all straight now. No chance of a backfire later. You're the elected spokesman, Kardell, and you set the price at a hundred dollars a gallon for all you've got. Yes!"

He rumpled up his tunic, his hands groping under it, unbuckling his money-belt, bringing it out. The money-belt hung in his hand, broad and thick, shaped by wear to the curve of his waist, its sweat-limbered leather embossed by the octagonal edges of gold coins stuffed into four of the pockets. The stitched seam of the big middle pocket had burst apart, from the pressure of overloading, exposing the edge of a hard wad of banknotes. It was the money-belt of a gambler who made no use of commercial banking facilities because banks were stationary and he was transient.

He slapped it against the boot of his good leg. They stared at it, probably thinking he was carrying the payroll to the Fort Laramie garrison. Despite whatever low hope they held of escape, the greed of money fired just the same glint in their eyes that it did in the eyes of wallies and layers and tinhorns anywhere.

"I'll buy," Laish said.

He saw the puzzled wonder in Kardell's face, and heard Tillotson's thin grunt of warning. Tillotson, foreseeing the direction of this unexpected turn, was sending his urgent message to Kardell to queer the deal. No sale. There was never meant to be a sale. The price should have prohibited it. But here the money showed, plain as gold dust in the scales. Cash. A heap more of it than any Army officer could be expected to tote around. Nobody could have guessed it.

Kardell's quandary flushed up an angry perplexity into his face, and finally a sullen balkiness. He hungered for the money, but he couldn't take it on the terms that he had set so confidently. In a minute, under Tillotson's pressing stare at him, he found a clumsy shift and growled at Laish, "It's two hundred a gallon!"

The muttering protests of the listening emigrants enraged him. They held to fair dealing. You set a price, you stuck to it.

"The price is gone up!" he snarled, as much at them as at Laish. "It's two hundred! Take it or leave it! Hell, it's our whisky, ain't it?"

Above a muttering, an Illinois farmer shouted, "Crawfish!"

Raising a hand for silence, Laish said reasonably, "That's pretty steep, Kardell. I've got no guarantee you won't get steeper, if I take it."

He had the emigrants swung over to him. That made a winning trick. Human emotions packed power. The sense of justice gathered an emotional quality that outweighed mere logic.

He happened to glance at the spread blanket again, at the cards held in the hands of the men who had been gambling, and an old mischief got into him. He knew that this was what he had been steering for: a gamble. He said to Kardell, "For a compromise, I'll make a gamble with you. We'll cut the cards—two hundred a gallon or nothing! Well?"

He watched both Tillotson and Kardell, while he swung the money-belt casually, flaunting it before them; the come-on. No capper ever could bunco a game alive more surely than a gilt-edged shill, the careless display of cash, the bait. The wallies fell for it every time. It dazzled them. It turned cynics into eager optimists.

Yet Tillotson still wanted to call off the whole thing. His long jaw worked nervously, betraying him. But he couldn't think of any way to call it off, and couldn't signal Kardell any line to take. The working of his jaw brought out a dry, thin sound of gritting teeth.

Kardell stood under pressure. The muttered scorn of the emigrants. The almost embarrassed expectancy of the crew. Tillotson's unspoken warning. The rich lure of the money-belt. They all conspired to put him into a dilemma, and again he took a wary shift. "If you're callin' for a gamble," he parried, "I got the right to name the game. Stud poker. Blind."

"Stud? Blind?" Laish drew his brows together. "How d'you play that one?"

"Why, we deal one card each, face down. That's the hole-card. It's— Ain't you ever played blind stud?" Kardell's enthusiasm increased visibly. "The hole-card is blind, meanin' we don't look at it. We make our bets on the other four cards 'cordin' as they fall, face up. We don't tip the hole-card till the showdown."

"You call that poker? Nothing but a game of chance and luck, no brains required!"

"With the bets at two hundred dollars a jug," declared Kardell, "I'm willin' to lean on luck an' leave the brains to you!"

Laish shrugged. "Very well, if children's games satisfy you." Turning to King, he inquired, "Do you happen to have a pack of cards on you? Those are filthy that they've been using."

"What? No, sir!" By his tone King announced his abysmal dismay. No doubt he had taken a trimming once, from some nimble-fingered operator. West Point disapproved, rightly, but most cadets passed through the deadfall initiation sooner or later, and some it cured for life. Unhappily, experience and superior knowledge gave rank to no shavetail to lecture the commanding general. He could only stand by in mute distress while the general made a fool of himself by blundering into a gaff that would spook a plebe.

"If what the boys got don't suit your fancy, I got another deck here," said Kardell, slipping a pack from his pocket. "These is near new, you can see." He fanned them out deftly.

Laish glanced at them. "They'll do," he allowed, and King opened his mouth and shut it again and the emigrants shook their heads in dismal pity. "Still, they're your cards," Laish said as an afterthought, "so I claim the deal. That's right, eh?"

"Right enough, sojer. Fair an' square's my aim!" Kardell handed over the cards, his private and unbeatable deck of fish-backs, wedged and nailed for those special occasions when a duck flew in. The general was a rare bird, ripe for rich plucking. With those cards, whoever dealt, nobody won but Kardell. Nobody else *could* win. The duck didn't stand a chance.

CHAPTER 10

LAISH AND KARDELL squatted on their heels, facing each other across the blanket on the ground. The men of the crew drew back, trying to hide grins, and the emigrants watched in dour silence. King looked as if he wanted to shout out to the trustful general, warning him to watch out for low tricks.

Shuffling, Laish busheled the cards twice. The first time, he frowned severely at the dropped cards and gathered them up, obviously displeased with their behavior. The second time, he muttered, "Damned fingers are stiff!" and stretched the fingers of his left hand, batting impatiently at the bandage on his forearm.

Kardell nodded, indulgent, looking on blandly. It didn't matter much what the duck dealt or how long he took about it. The cards were readers, accurately marked. The hole-card was the stinger, and as long as you could read what it was, from its back, you were sure of plucking the duck.

The cards were thumbnailed on the cross-and-dot system, Laish observed as he clumsily shuffled. That old system. As raw as stripping and edge-work. Almost as raw as the table-bug and the sleeve-clip, devices of the cheap tinhorn. He dealt.

By their nail-marks, the hole-cards told bad news for

Laish. His was the deuce of hearts, Kardell's the ace of diamonds. But they were blind, face down. Ostensibly, nobody knew what they were.

The next cards, dealt face up, placed him low—the queen of clubs, against the ace of spades for Kardell. Gently, Kardell made a bet, laying one match down on the blanket in lieu of a jug. Laish threw in a match and flipped up the seven of hearts for Kardell, the five of diamonds to himself. Still nursing it along, Kardell checked. Laish passed. No bet.

The fourth round gave Kardell the ace of clubs, Laish the queen of spades.

Now it looked interesting. Kardell, with his pair of aces showing against Laish's pair of queens, shoved in two matches. Laish hesitated, put in his two, and when he completed the deal it changed the show completely. He drew the queen of diamonds, giving him three queens. Kardell got the seven of diamonds, making two pairs showing for him, sevens and aces; not counting his blind ace in the hole.

"Nice deal," Kardell remarked, stretching his thick arms and yawning largely, while cocking another look at the marked hole-cards to make dead sure he was due to win. "You're high—three queens. It's your bet."

Threes, beating two pairs, were worth money. They cropped up about once in seventy, on the average, in a pat hand in draw poker. The odds ran even higher in stud, discounting the hole-card. A hundred to one, or thereabouts. Three queens were worth money. You bet on them. In a two-hand game you bet your shirt on them and that was good poker.

Laish asked, "Did we set a limit here? I don't recall that we did."

"No, we didn't," Kardell answered brightly. He scanned

the marked backs of the hole-cards once more. He couldn't possibly lose. His was the ace of diamonds, filling his hand. Laish's was the deuce of hearts, a rag. "You wanna bet high? We-ell, now, I feel lucky. I ain't no short-sport. Bet 'em high an' sleep in the streets—that's me! How much? Throw it all in, sojer!"

"All, you say? I'll take you up on that!" Laish thumped his money-belt on the blanket, sweeping aside the matches. "There's my bet, b'gahd!"

"The whole pile, huh?" Kardell purred.

"As much of it as covers your rotgut whisky, yes! Let's get done with this damned nonsense!"

It was spoken like a bluntly forthright soldier whose self-confidence far outstretched his patience for picayune betting with matchsticks.

Kardell grinned around at the emigrants, at the wagon crew, and at King, who stood crucified by shame and anguish. And at Tillotson, who nodded his understanding and assent. "I call you!" he notified Laish.

He turned up his hole-card. "Well, looka that!" he crowed, somewhat overdoing his feigned surprise. "I hit the long-shot! Three aces, two sevens! I got a full house!" He reached hungrily for the money-belt.

"I've got—"

Laish made his fumble. He scattered his top cards, slapped irritably at his bandages, and finally got his hole-card exposed. "Ah, here she is—the modest lady of the quartette. Four queens beat your full, my friend. Yes, a nice deal!"

Too nice. It skipped the laws of probability, and juggled the evidence of eyes. Kardell glared incredulously at that fourth queen. Slowly the knowledge penetrated: Laish had somehow pulled a switch.

He couldn't base a claim on it, couldn't bawl out that

he knew Laish's hole-card had been a deuce. An admission of using marked cards, even though everybody guessed they were marked, didn't exactly put a man on solid ground for complaint when somebody worked them against him. But he did know, as surely as he had known that his own hole-card was an ace. Frustration and impotence corroded his sense; he felt for his knife, rising.

Laish buckled his money-belt back on, saying briskly to King, "Help me go through these wagons, please! Any whisky in them is mine, and I claim the right to search for my property. There certainly should be no objections to that, from anybody, don't you think so?"

"N—No, sir. Yes, sir. I—uh—should suppose not, under the—uh—the circumstances!"

Rumbling laughter confirmed the suppositio Not all the listening emigrants laughed; many looked askance at low gambling tricks, especially when practiced by a high-ranking Army officer. But on the whole their sentiments favored the Army against civilians, this once.

Tillotson, weighing all that, said frozenly, "No objections, General. You are within your rights, of course." He drew a deep breath, and his eyes flashed dully. "You guessed correctly. There is a full wagon load of whisky. That wagon there." He motioned at the wagon under which the skinny man with the rifle crouched.

Laish nodded. "Yes, I guessed it. Trade whisky. For your Sioux customers on Green River, eh? Red Cloud's mob, most likely. What some of you traders will do for a profit! I should think it would occur to you that a wagon load of whisky, for the Sioux, might be reason enough for Rasakura's Pawnees to attack this emigrant train!"

Tillotson heard him through without interrupting. "It has occurred to me," he murmured, dry-lipped. "The whisky is now yours. It's your responsibility. I am glad to be rid of it."

"Very well. You're rid of it. King, have that wagon cut out and placed under guard." Laish shifted his attention to Kardell, scanning him carefully.

Kardell was both heavy and agile, with the elaborate pose so often affected by barroom toughs and ugly drunks. He tilted his head high as he came erect, gave Laish a raking once over, and complained in an injured tone, "Now, looka here—I own a share in that whisky wagon, Gen'ral!"

It was probably true. Allowing the top wagon-man a stake in the trade made one way of clinching his loyalty. It was also probably true that Kardell owned the crew, or at least stood as its undisputed leader. He had said so, and the crew had not thrown in a single protesting vote. The hard drinking had gone on simply because Tillotson could not stop it, Laish judged. Tillotson didn't have control of his outfit. Kardell held the reins and cracked the whip over the crew, and his bloodshot stare showed the reckless mood of an unmanageable drunkard.

"I'm a poor man, an' sick!" Kardell shuffled forward slowly, in his revolting mimicry of cringing humbleness, one forefinger plucking at his lower lip. This evidently marked a recognized prelude. The crew was a silent and absorbed audience.

Kardell ignored Tillotson's worried face. The skinny man under the whisky wagon humped up on one elbow, lined up the sights of his rifle, drew a deliberate bead on Laish. And smiled, baring broken teeth. A rum-head.

"Wouldn't skin a poor sick man, Gen'ral, wouldja?"

Kardell was almost within reach. The transparent humility thinned off. His eyes glowed a crazy merriment.

Laish heard King's whisper: "Watch out, sir—his knife! His left hand!"

He let Kardell advance one more step, and told him, "I'm taking the whisky. Nothing will change that. Understand? Nothing!"

"Do say!"

Kardel whipped his left hand around and forward. The point of the long blade scraped Laish's gun belt and tugged up the front of his blue tunic, coming to halt just over the abdomen. It was the position for instant thrust, sword fashion, endorsed by the butcher-knife boys.

"Do say! How's this, you yallerleg son of a—"

The coat flew apart, heavy Colt's gun barrel upper-cutting the hand and knife. The knife clanged loose from Kardell's broken grip, batted aloft. The gun, continuing its upswing, grazed his face. It routed him back a stumbling half-step, to striking distance, and then its full downsweep sledged him.

The essence of Laish's action amounted only to a simple up-and-down stroke. For surprise, it depended upon the sleight-of-hand draw. While Kardell's knees buckled, Laish cut a shot over him at the man under the whisky wagon. The skinny man dropped his rifle and hung his head, bowed against the wagon wheel. Nobody else moved.

At last Tillotson, staring strangely at Laish, exclaimed, "General?" in a tone choked by sheer disbelief. They were all staring at him in that same way, King too.

He had made a very bad slip, the worst one yet by far. There had been no good way to avoid it, he told himself. But it was bad. He felt them still staring after him when he left. On his limping course through the big wagon corral he grew conscious of all eyes following him.

He saw Mignon and Reverend Yount, and Carqueville and others, evidently returning from the Arab's funeral. They had paused, and must have witnessed at least part of the affair. Mignon gazed at him, her eyes enormous, and

she suddenly turned as if to run away. It was Private Carqueville, swiftly at her side, who offered his arm. Mignon
took it, and Carqueville led her out of sight around a
long picket line of horses. She seemed quite shaken, Laish
noted. Trembling all over. Shuddering, rather.

He saw Christella in a group of silent, white-faced
women. She had been looking at him, he was sure, but
her eyes avoided his. She walked away, toward that good
wagon of hers, hurrying, in the manner of a shy girl not
wishing to be spoken to by him.

God, was it that bad? Had it appeared that brutal, ruthless, murderous? Couldn't they see he had only done what
needed doing, and done it with the tools he knew best how
to use?

"I wish," he muttered drearily, "I'd taken the trail to
Santa Fe, and to hell with the patrols!"

Croshaw, presently joining Laish in the canvas shelter,
put the thing into plain words. "Well, you sure showed
your bronco brand!" he remarked, sitting on his heels.
"Call me a bigmouth—an' you pull a sizzler like that!"

"Would you have elected Yount to take it on?" Laish
demanded sourly.

"Kardell's a goner," Croshaw said. "So's the other'n.
It was a gunfighter's trick. An' that game—yeah, you
showed 'em! You braced Kardell. You slicked him neat.
Stacked the cards. Ev'rybody's got that figgered now. How
long did you ever last, any place you lit, 'fore you had to
dust out on the high lope?"

"That," Laish responded, "is none of your damned business! Don't let your mouth lead you astray, sagebrusher!"

"They're sayin' you acted just like a cardshark an' a
killer—an' looked it! Fact is, you still got that funny kind
o' look." Croshaw slapped his palms on his knees, and

straightened up from squatting. "Mister, it won't do! You better watch it!"

"Are you trying to give me orders?"

"No. But we made a bargain, remember." Squinting off at something, Croshaw added, "Don't you reckon you coulda let the lieutenant handle that squabble? He wanted to, but you took it on yourself. I reckon I know why you did."

Laish shoved himself up onto his elbows. Following the direction of the guide's look, he saw Christella and King together near the girl's wagon. "You think King could've handled that set-up? You think he's big enough?"

"Yeah," replied Croshaw. "I think he'll do." He brought his faded eyes back to Laish, a cool knowledge lurking in their pale depths. "You're big, sure. You're a ring-tailed curly wolf, an' in a scrape you're the best I ever met. But in some ways you won't do, mister! Not a-tall!"

The word he used was "Mister." Not "Gen'ral."

He had served under Pepper Andy. He didn't think that a man wearing Pepper Andy's star should ever behave like a gambler and gunfighter. He thought Laish should be given to know that, and to understand that he should yank his attention off a real nice girl. Miss Brunk wasn't any dance-hall dame. Not by a hell-sight. Nor a flighty young widow, come to that.

"You go to hell!" Laish grunted. "Kindly inform Lieutenant King for me that we move out tonight. It'll surprise him. He probably thinks we're here to plant a crop!"

That was unfair to King, he realized, so he said, "Tell him we've got to push on. No water here and not enough grass for the animals. He can understand. So can you."

"Sure," Croshaw agreed. "Your judgment's right every time. I don't find no fault there." He glanced again toward Christella's wagon. "I'll tell him. In a minute. No rush, is there?"

Laish sat up. "Kelly!" he called to his runner.

He searched his pockets and found the stub of a pencil. From the folds of the bandage on his arm he snapped out the deuce of diamonds, and scrawled on it: *Make ready move on tonight early*. He handed it to Private Kelly.

"To Lieutenant King. Immediately."

Kelly hurried off with it, and Laish said to Croshaw, "Let him understand that, dammit! And you, too!"

Croshaw left without comment.

CHAPTER 11

THE LEADING WAGONS began angling cautiously down the slopes soon after dark, huge wheels crackling and loose ironware jangling.

It wasn't possible to make all these emigrant families tie down and muffle their household goods. Kettles and washtubs banged outside, harness-brasses clinked, and inside the wagons a thousand objects nudged merrily together, half of them useless, all cherished from the torn-up homes left far behind.

And it didn't much matter in the long run anyway. The spying Indians quickly knew of every move the train made, and on their fast ponies they could catch up with it any time they pleased. The only advantage against them was their ingrained reluctance to fight at night. Outside of that, they held all the cards. The emigrant train was the bull buffalo lumbering westward; the Indians were the fleet wolves. The likeness grew closer every hour.

The hopelessness of this cumbersome flight was a dead weight crushing the vigor and spirit of the whole train. It stamped a sullen dejection on all faces. Among the emigrant people it inflamed festers of muttering rebellion. By their dismal silence, troopers betrayed their uneasiness over abandoning the campsite.

Everybody was worn out, that was the trouble. Laish

would not let them rest and he could not be forever ex-plaining to them the necessity to push on. He knew the fatal risk of resting, of allowing time for an enemy to re-cover from a setback. These people also knew it, deep within—but weariness urged rest, wait, stay forted.

"Same order of march as before," Laish told King, "ex-cept that I want Sergeant Lybarger back with me. And that whisky wagon of Tillotson's will travel in the rear with us where his crew can't get at it. Don't let the column get spread out, up at your end. Some of these people are contrary."

King acknowledged the order and said, "There is some disaffection." And he meant, as Laish knew, that the Til-lotson affair had produced repercussions. Although Tillot-son's men had aroused angry hostility by their behavior, there was a feeling that General Pepperis had overstepped all bounds in his handling of them.

"Yes, I heard Reverend Yount's funeral oration over Kardell and that other hoodlum," Laish remarked, a bit dryly. " 'Imperious tyranny. Ruthless terrorism. Heathen cynicism—' I thought at first he was speaking of the Apaches! You have something to ask me?"

"The confiscated Tillotson wagon, sir. Could you in-form me of the procedure in entering a thousand gallons of whisky—more or less—in the Report?"

Laish grinned. He thought he saw humor in King's eyes, and just for that moment they were two men sharing an appreciation of the comic side of formality. Then he saw that he was mistaken. King was serious. There was nothing funny about it in King's mind.

"I won the whisky, King," Laish said solemnly. "It is not necessary to enter our winnings at cards, if any, in the Report. It would only confuse the Department, I'm sure!"

As the circle of wagons gradually uncurled and strung out, each white-top rocked gigantically into the glow of the distant Indian fires before pitching on down the slopes. At the foot, the train bent west, away from the fires and out onto the floor of the open plains. This was a test of nerves—the act of forsaking shelter, exchanging it for the shelterless unknown.

Laish glanced at each passing wagon, and when the one came along that he was waiting for he rode on beside it.

As once before, he touched his hat and said, "Good evening."

He wished he were driving that wagon, with her at his side. The wish raced on, but the darkness hid the direct message in his eyes. He listened to her quiet voice give back is greeting.

"How is your knee?" Christella asked.

His knee was all right, he told her. He had it heavily padded. Riding was not too uncomfortable. It would be stiff for a long time, yes, and perhaps leave him with a limp. It could have been worse.

Then he heard her say, with feeling, "Reverend Yount talked like a fool today, and I told him so!"

The wagon lurched down onto level ground and swung west with the column. Able then to slack off the lines, Christella leaned back tiredly on the seat. She said, "Necessity knows no law. The greater good for the greater number. I recognized that, after a little thought. Your killing of those two men was a bad thing—but by their own actions they made it a necessity. It was as necessary as the killing of enemy Indians. What made it bad was— It's hard to put into words. The way you did it. The way you looked. I suppose it was especially the way you looked."

She had Mignon on her mind, he thought. She said,

"And yet, when a man sets out to kill another man, for good reason—or for what he believes is good reason—he can't be expected to look like a saint. You looked like a devil!"

"Perhaps," he suggested, "it was the way I felt."

She shook her head. "No. You did it like a devil, too, but—no. I told Reverend Yount to remember what you have done and are doing for all of us. Reverend Yount retorted that it was no more than should be expected of an Army officer, and that you were paid to do your duty."

"That fixed you, eh?"

"Yes. That fixed me!" she laughed softly. "It was frustrating. I couldn't very well contradict him, could I? And that was when I lost my temper and told him he was a fool."

With a return to her quiet tone, she asked, "How much chance is there, really? Won't the Indians follow us onto open ground? Won't they attack all the harder?"

"Yes, of course," Laish said. "But with luck, this train will get to Fort Laramie. With luck, I repeat—for your ears only."

She accepted that and asked further, "What will be done to *you* there at Fort Laramie, if we reach it?"

The answer to that was too easy. In his brief Army career, alone, he reflected, he had somehow managed to run up a considerable score, not counting the impersonation of an officer. He didn't care to delve into that.

"I'll get past Fort Laramie—with luck!"

He smiled at Christella, and dropped back.

He had been wrong about Pepper Troop. It was not yet run out. It had taken a terrible mauling in the sandhills, but it was still on tap.

Thirty-one strong, the men followed the last wagon

down the slopes in a ragtail procession which even Sergeant Lybarger hadn't the heart to yank into order. More than half of them had wounds and hurts to curse softly over, and some could have ridden in the wagons with the litter wounded.

The riderless horses were led along loosely, supposedly as spare mounts. Mostly it was because of a feeling that the empty-saddle horses belonged in Pepper Troop, like the wounded men, and wouldn't feel right elsewhere.

"Snuffy lot o' donks!" growled Sergeant Lybarger, and Laish wasn't sure whether he meant the men or the horses.

Lybarger's next comment made it clear. "Two-three them jockeys, sir, they had to be lifted on, they're that damaged. I told 'em to muck off this detail. They told me to go squat on my lousy rank! What'll I do about 'em, sir?"

"Pick them up gently, Sergeant, if they fall off."

"Yes, sir."

For a moment Sergeant Lybarger sat stiffly on his horse, not comfortable, wanting words with which to set himself straight on record.

"With the General's leave, sir, I'd like to mention I—" he began, and there he got embarrassingly lost. In the end, he said, "It's a good outfit—troop, I mean, sir. This troop, sir."

It was as close as he could come to saying right out that he was proud to be sergeant of this straggling bunch of banged-up junipers. Other things were implied, too.

"We're glad to have you back here with us, Sergeant," Laish told him. "Let's hook a jug out of that wagon and pass it around, eh?"

A short while later, Laish said, "Halt that wagon, Sergeant, and take the teams off. We'll leave it right here where they can't miss it."

Looking startled, Sergeant Lybarger exclaimed, "Them

139

sir?" He swept an arm back at the Indian fires.

"Yes. Leave it here for them. Break a jug, so the stink spreads down the breeze. That trade whisky's got a stink nobody could mistake. Certainly not an Indian!"

Lybarger rode on into the darkness, and Laish heard him speak to the wagon driver. The whisky wagon slowed to a standstill. Laish halted the troop, and while waiting he weighed the risk of what he was doing.

That load of trade whisky was a tempting prize to Indians, and perhaps it was the prize that they had been striving for all along. Their main objective. They could have got wind of it before it ever cleared the Bull Creek settlements. A careless remark, made by one of Tillotson's hoodlums perhaps, and picked up by someone such as that silently listening old Pawnee who hung around Owsley's roadhouse. Or some prowling thief who had sneaked a look in the night and whispered of what he saw. Maybe that hungry kid.

Logic insisted that there had to be a very good reason for Pawnees to discard their allegiance to the whites, to turn renegade, to institute a ruthless campaign to capture a wagon train. They did love whisky, and that could be the reason. White men, too, driven by that same thirst, had been known to commit bloody crimes.

Somebody interrupted the work of Sergeant Lybarger and the driver at the whisky wagon. Lybarger's growl could be heard in response to a question, and a rider walked his horse on toward the halted troop and drew in before Laish.

It was Tillotson. He inquired tonelessly, "General, what do you propose doing with my wagon?"

"I'm leaving it behind," Laish told him. "If it's whisky they're after, they can have it!"

He rather hoped that the trader would raise strenuous

objections, and so he put snap into his tone. "That kind of merchandise has no right to freight with an emigrant wagon! You know it! We're not fighting to protect whisky runners!"

Tillotson's eyes glimmered curiously in the darkness. "As far as the whisky is concerned, I say good riddance. It was bought by Kardell and some of the drivers for their own trading ventures. I had to agree or be left stranded without a crew. If you think the stuff is responsible for all our trouble, by all means leave it. The wagon is mine, though. My wagons are specially built, and they cost—"

"We haven't time to unload!"

Again Tillotson failed to protest. He inclined his head in agreement and said placatingly, "Let the wagon go, then."

Loose chains dragged jinglingly on the ground as the teams separated from the wagon. There was the sharp crash of a jug smashed on the iron tire of a wheel. Tillotson turned his face toward the sound and brought it back inquiringly to Laish.

"For the smell," Laish explained. "For Indian bait."

"Oh." Tillotson nodded. Then he said in the toneless voice he had used previously, "I have seen mad-drunk Indians." And he shivered, seeming to hunch down and grow small. "A few. Not *that* many! Not the crowd that we've got against us!"

There he put his finger accurately on the risk, with a coward's instant perception. It was the vivid reality of the risk, whipping his imagination, that drained him of the ability to fire up anger. The glimmer of his staring eyes mirrored the naked horror of his visions, and for an instant Laish could imagine all that Tillotson was seeing. Berserk howlers, drunkenly fearless, sweeping through the column, cutting it to pieces. Then the orgy of lust, blood, burnings—the massacre.

A bit quickly, Laish said, "You've also seen dead-drunk Indians, haven't you?"

He looked at the wagon, and so did Tillotson.

"Frankly, I don't know if that's what they're after. I don't know what getting it will do to them. There's plenty of whisky for all of them there. I'm gambling they'll get drunk. And stay here drunk until they've finished the load. If I'm wrong—well, we won't be any worse off than we are."

"I suppose not," Tillotson said, reining off. "I hope not. With all my soul, I hope you are right!" He sounded skeptical, but he was a yellow buzzard and you couldn't look to his kind for bright hopes on a long gamble.

When Lybarger reported his task done, Laish got the feeling that the sergeant for once was inclined to share Tillotson's pessimism. The men, after they realized that the whisky was actually being abandoned to the Indians, did considerable belly-aching. They trooped reluctantly past the stalled whisky wagon, looked constantly back until the darkness hid it, and sank into a gloomy silence.

If this gamble went bad, Laish guessed, there would be few to excuse him and many to condemn him. And the worst of it was, he knew he would condemn himself. Already doubts were pricking him and again he glimpsed Tillotson's hideous visions.

With a word to Lybarger, he put his horse to a lope and rode up the line to Christella's wagon.

"Do you have a gun of some kind?" he asked Christella.

The harsh abruptness of his question brought a long look from her, a look of ready understanding that acknowledged fear but no panic. And her voice was like that, very grave, very calm, asking him in return, "Are our chances lost?"

"I can't say. I've done something that"—he spoke care-

142

fully now—"may turn the trick for us. It may not. To play to win, in anything, one should be prepared to lose." He returned her steady look. He was sodden with weariness and pain and suddenly he could not go further.

She knew his meaning. "There's a pistol in my father's trunk. I know how to fire it."

"Load it, please, and keep it by you from now on. Will you?"

"Yes, of course."

She was so much younger than he, yet it was as if she leaned over him from a wise height of understanding and gentleness. "But I don't believe I'll need it. I believe you will—turn the trick!"

"Thank you," he said. This was what he had needed. He had not known how much he needed the few words of confidence. "Thank you, Christella."

The column marched west. Its rate settled to a fair three miles an hour on the level plain. As the fires of the hostile Indian camps receded hourly and dimmed down, to that degree the spirits of the emigrant train and the Army escort rose as inevitably as the outweighed scale-pan of a delicate balance. Nobody believed the menace was gone, but the withdrawn signs of its presence was a relief that could not help bringing forth a lifting optimism. They hoped so desperately.

The outguard files reported seeing no Indian scouts for a long while. Then, drivers began calling neighborly to one another in nearly normal voices, and the women retreated inside their wagons to get some sleep with the quieted children. The riding troopers drifted into revery, solemn or fantastic according to mind and mood—that fortunate affliction of riders in the long night, induced by darkness and the undisturbed rhythm of a horse, and man's persistent inner life.

The column marched all night with the risen moon, and in the morning everybody knew that this day at least they would have peace.

Under the great kettle of blue sky the prairie spread out flat and empty, a calm ocean of grass, on and on to the purple mist of the horizon, where the evidence of eyes insisted that it must melt into eternal space. Nothing existed there, west, north, south. No landmark, boundary, or topographical hazard to place a definite question before the imagination. Only by gazing back, eastward, could the seeking eyesight find the comfort of focus, for there ran the bold ruts of the wagon wheels, following the train.

There were no Indians, not a solitary sign of one.

And Laish grinned at last.

His grin had to crack through the gray exhaustion stamped on his beard-stubbled, dirty face, and it came out as a cadaverous grimace. He was in rags, knees and elbows burst out of breeches and sleeves, the rags foul with dried sweat and grime and dust. He had given up brushing the flies off the caked bandages. The need of rest was a hunger fevering him, and he felt that his bloodshot eyeballs were imbedded in gritty sockets. But he sat there, grinning at the empty east, until Sergeant Lybarger and Hoback helped him off his horse.

He let himself down slowly on the blanket that they spread for him, muttering, "By God, it worked!" And they were grinning, too.

"How did you do it, sir?" That was Lieutenant King, very respectful, very concerned for him. King, coming in properly to see to the morning report. The train was circling to halt, to make camp.

"How did you work it, sir?"

Laish snorted a laugh. *Me—military genius!*

"Rasakura," he said, already half asleep, "couldn't get 'em past that bootleg wagon!"

Croshaw's chuckle rang out, and King said, "Please accept my congratulations, sir! Finest delaying maneuver since Hippomenes tossed gold apples to the virgin Atalanta!" King was young. That classic thought came naturally to him.

And there was Croshaw, saying, "Pawnees, Shoshones, Crows, Sacs—and them 'Paches. All that firewater! It ought to be boilin' 'em all up in a hot scrap back there by now! Wonder did the general count on that? You reckon he did, Lieutenant?"

Too worn to open his eyes and respond, Laish thought druggedly, *You don't know me! I turned the trick!*

Nobody, after this, would doubt his judgment or murmur at his actions, whatever he did. He was running the whole damned show, running it right. Croshaw had better keep a tight check-rein on his tongue. Take care of him. Take care of everything. He wasn't beat, not by a damned sight.

CHAPTER 12

T HAT DAY the train really rested. There was a general letdown of cruelly strained nerves, a grateful sense of release as the sun topped the sky and brought afternoon heat, and the world around stayed empty.

The care of the wounded and sick, the doctoring of stock, repairs to wagons and harness, a multitude of chores cropped up to hold back the start of that night's march. Everything needed doing, everybody maintaining that his particular chore was essential. For some of the women, life was unthinkable if they didn't get out a washing. Common tasks reassumed their high importance.

Too willing to believe the danger past, many of the emigrants favored giving up the night march. Laish had some inclination to agree, being in hard shape, but Croshaw argued too positively against it.

"One day don't signify to a drunk Injun! Like as not, tomorrow they'll be whoopin' all around us. We gotta keep this outfit rollin'! You can't lay down now, man!"

So they got off to a late start and rolled a few miles to sunup. But not the next night, for by then nobody short of Rasakura himself could have refuted the jubilant belief that the hostiles had quit.

The third day dawning on empty horizons, even Croshaw did not object much to a return to daily routine, and the train crunched along once more in blazing sunlight. What Croshaw did object to was Laish's refusal to send forward to Fort Laramie for reinforcements. He led up to the subject in roundabout fashion, the fourth day from the whisky wagon, by giving Laish a bit of confidential advice as to his future.

"At Bernard, this side o' Laramie, there's a trail that drops south way down to Taos and Santa Fe. Carson useta drive sheep over it. Yeah, ol' Kit. If I was you, that's the trail I'd have in mind," said Croshaw.

Twice today he had happened along on his undersized mare, and coolly joined Laish, riding alongside Christella's wagon.

"If it all goes right," he said, "tomorrow we cross the Punkinseed. You foller the creek, then slant southwest, an' you oughta strike that trail somewhere down near the Lodgepole."

"You mean I should quit the train?"

"You got to, ain't you? Fort Laramie—"

"Yes, I know."

The glint was in Laish's eyes. Was this meddling little cuckoo spouting out the law? Giving orders?

"But we're still about five days yet from Laramie, my friend. I don't see myself coursing a hundred miles 'cross-country, searching for a sheep track to Santa Fe. I will quit this train in my own time!"

Squinting down his pointed nose, Croshaw said doggedly, "We'll be sendin' on to Laramie for troops to meet us. It shoulda been done before this. Lots of them ol' Laramie bowlegs—specially the officers—know Pepper Andy by sight! If you ain't gone when they meet us—"

"They won't meet us!" Laish said.

It was anger, as much as anything, that brought that out. And once it was out, Laish perceived the shape of the future. For him, Fort Laramie was a hazard, an impossible one.

For King it was also an obstacle. King would be stuck there, for weeks, probably months, waiting for orders transferring him to some other station. The emigrant train would travel on west to Oregon. Farewell to Lieutenant Joyce King and company. You did a splendid job and we will always remember you in our prayers.

"We will not be sending for troops from Fort Laramie, Croshaw. We don't need them now."

The faded blue eyes of the civilian guide belonged all at once to a stern man, to a man who was not drab and scraggly and limp.

"Mister, yer goin' wrong on me! I don't like it! Your aim is to stick till the last night, an' slip on 'round Laramie, eh? West o' Laramie, you'd pick up a change o' wear. You'd lay up at La Prelle or Deer Creek ferry, or maybe the Gap, to join this outfit again when it came through, eh?"

"That's about it."

"So I thought! An' 'spose the hostiles take another crack before we get to Laramie? They might. Damn it, man, yer gamblin' the whole train on yer own personal game!"

Laish felt his face stiffen and darken warmly. "The hostiles have quit! That wagon load of whisky turned the trick. I won that gamble and I'll win the next! I'll be with this train when it reaches Oregon!"

"They won't have you! You're a bogus, an' they'll know it an' they'll run you off!"

"You're a liar," Laish said. "Nobody knows me in Oregon."

He watched Croshaw's eyes, watched for the knife. At some point, Croshaw was quite likely to flash up without an instant's warning, if convinced of his rightness.

"My credit is high with these people. They won't condemn me for fighting without pay in a borrowed uniform. I've done enough for them to excuse that."

"If you don't send on to Fort Laramie for troops," Croshaw promised grimly, "yer credit don't shine for me a dam'! I know yer game! I don't string with it! Not at all!"

"Try to cross me up, would you?" Laish nodded. "I think you would!"

"I warned you at the start, back on the Platte! Go wrong on me, I said, and I'll get you!"

"So you did. Yes." Laish's glance picked out Christella's wagon. He let his voice drop to a murmur. "I give you as straight a warning, my friend! You may spike my plans. I may have to bolt off down to Santa Fe, and perhaps clear to Old Mexico, with a Laramie squad on my tracks. But when this caravan finally makes Oregon, I'll be with it again—or I'll be there soon after! And you'll be a dead man, much as I dislike the thought of killing you!"

Croshaw eyed him searchingly—almost, it seemed, in grudging admiration of his cool gall. Then he looked upward and said to the sky, "One of us'll be, for sure!"

The heavy wagon wheels scored on westward, that day and the next, and another morning saw them through the abrupt sandstone temples and castles of the Bluffs and lined out on the straight haul toward Fort Laramie. Except for divergences here and there, made necessary by the terrain, the caravan now followed the North Platte. The riverbed narrowed steadily, but its banks remained sandy and barren. The stream kept to the general appearance of the lower Platte, streaky; bright green willows growing from tiny islands of pale sand gave a false illusion of foliage flourishing in rich soil.

A massive and fantastic freak of natural landscaping, the Bluffs. Their lowest extremity curved like the end of a gigantic shepherd's crook, and from that they towered into an isolated pile of pillars and gaunt minarets and buttressed walls that might have been built by a race of ancient gods who eventually found the world too small for their vast scale of measurement. The Bluffs awed all travelers of the plains. Past them, nobody could help feeling that the worst was behind.

Forward-looking and eager, the emigrant drivers struck their best gait and trundled out of line to pass slower neighbors, and the column strung two miles long from head to rearguard. Watch had grown lax in the lasting lack of anything to watch out for. Discipline fell to an easygoing semblance of order. Fort Laramie lay ahead, with armed escorts fresh and strong from there on. Oregon or bust—and it wouldn't be bust. This train had fought through the toughest Indian menace. It was bound to get there.

A routine detail of a dozen troopers ambled far in the rear, clear of the dust, occasionally remembering to glance perfunctorily around. Croshaw and Lieutenant King rode up forward at the head, where they belonged by order of the commander. The escort files paid hawk-heed to the younger emigrant women and girls of the train, and Laish's horse had learned to match its walk perfectly to that of Christella's team.

Since the Tillotson affair, Laish had not exchanged a word with Mignon. She avoided even a greeting. Two or three times he caught sight of Carqueville pausing by her wagon, to salute, to speak a few words—Private Carqueville, so obviously an ex-officer of some proud army or other; ex-gentleman, scholar, student of the classics. A slim-waisted man, losing his dark and sunken lines of thorough-going dissipation, gaining hard leanness, keeping his personal sense of humor.

" '—The topless towers of Ilium!' " Laish heard him say when in sight of the Bluffs. And then to the appreciatively listening roughnecks around him: " *'Roll your tails, and roll 'em high!'* "—singing it in his excellent tenor—" *'We'll all be angels, by and by!'* "

The roughnecks loved it. Carky had been around. He knew a swad of funny sayings and songs. Could take care of himself, too. Lick any one of them in a fair scrap.

A very good trooper, Carqueville. It didn't weigh terribly about Mignon and him. There had been other affairs. Laish found that he was incapable of jealousy insofar as Mignon was concerned, and bitterness against Carqueville was out of the question. He was able to ask Christella, while riding alongside her wagon, "And how is Mrs. Pepperis?"

"She is well, I believe," Christella responded. "Better than I would have hoped, in fact, under these circumstances."

Her too-frank eyes said: *You fool! Mignon doesn't want to hurt you again, as she hurt you once before. She loves another man. But you are not lost. You are not alone again and wasted. A woman loves you, you fool! God in heaven, give him the sight to see it! I understand this man, to the deepest grain of his misguided soul. This gunfighting gambler, impostor, pretending he's a brigadier general—not for dollar gain, but to guide this mixed mob of land-seekers safely through the savage country.*

The Bluffs screened off the eastern horizon behind the long column of emigrant convoy and Army escort, and were themselves screened cloudily by the column's own dust.

Nobody saw the pursuing Indians until their dark mass was a blotch sharply outlined on the plain, giving the impression of having always been there. At that distance it took a minute or two for the Indians' forward movement to become perceptible. And then everybody in the caravan saw.

It must have been King who squalled the order to fort in. The head of the caravan—Tillotson's big freight wagons—bent to the right, to begin carving the circle, mounted soldiers plunging at the teams, hazing them to a run. Behind them the extended lines of emigrant wagons lurched into a chaotic chariot-race. Groups of walkers burst apart, running, scrambling onto their individual wagons, women screaming to their children.

This, Laish should have seen first, should have foreseen. Should certainly have seen before King, who was far forward. Too lax. Too occupied with purely personal involvements.

This was panic. The awful suddenness of it sucked everybody into the undertow of frantic fright, flight. It shrank every face: the utter collapse of security. This was his doing. He had not sent on to Fort Laramie for reinforcements.

On his headlong ride to the rearguard, Laish shouted for the escort files to round in after him. His mind retained for a little while the look in Christella's eyes, her white dismay, when she broke off midway through some remark.

He wondered if she, like Croshaw, condemned him for taking the chance and risking the whole train on his own gamble. His gamble seemed so petty now to him: slip around Fort Laramie and rejoin the train farther on west— a dodge, based on the assumption that the Indian menace was thrown off.

Here came the Indians, refuting his assumption, making a four-flusher of him, a blackleg tinhorn, a short-sport who wagered the other fellow's chips. He would never gamble again—if he lived.

"Sergeant Lybarger!"

"Sir?"

The rear scout detail clattered in, to report belatedly the presence of hostiles. Lybarger swore at them and threw them in with Pepper Troop. The men of the escort files crowded up, following Laish, exciting the horses, jostling like a mob of unruly cowhands. A young recruit accidentally touched off the trigger of his rifle. Hoback landed a punch on him, snarling, "Not in this outfit you don't!"

"Sergeant, we spread out for skirmish! What? Yes, yes—into line, guide center. And listen, all! We hold 'em off for as long as it takes the train to get forted in. We've done this before, some of us, haven't we?" Laish looked intently at faces grown familiar to him, the remnant of Pepper Troop, pinning on them the hope for hard bone to stiffen this uncertain body of men.

"We don't fall back till we're ready to!" he said to them. "We don't let ourselves get cut off, either!"

The faces of the troopers wore a single thought. *This was done before, sure—with the help of the sandhills and that 'boscado trick, and at the cost of damned near half the troop. This is different. The field of battle here is as bare as a parade ground, and what the hell can you do about it, General Pepperis? How do you stop a goddam flood?*

He didn't know. A trick was needed and he didn't have one to fit. He could lead them out, seventy-odd men against a thousand or more. The magic, if any, had to be theirs. They knew it.

Sergeant Lybarger let go at them with: "God help any you rooks who's slacked off carryin' his full issue of ammunition! No time now to tap the ammo wagon, an' the first one dry-shoots he's Injun bait!" To Laish, then, without the slightest hint of irony: "Has the gen'ral got any further orders, sir?"

It came to Laish that they were infantrymen, after all, and the infantry upheld its own proud traditions. He said, "We'd maybe have time to dig rifle pits. Infantry in rifle pits give Indians the horrors—they've never found a way to beat that trick. They'd have to pass around us. But that wouldn't help the wagon folks, would it?"

No, their faces said. You couldn't take the rifle pits along with you, when you fell back to fight for the train.

"So I guess we'll just have to play it out this way," he said. "Sergeant, let there be a squad in our rear. A dozen men or so. Let Carqueville—" He caught Carqueville's cool eye and nodded to him, and Carqueville nodded back. "Let *Corporal* Carqueville have charge of that squad. He will give us effective support wherever it will be needed, at his discretion. That is all."

And that was all it could be. Seventy-odd men walked their horses out rather sedately from the long dust-streamers of the circling wagons, to dispute the advance of an army of warriors who, being past-masters at fighting on the plains, could hardly have wished for anything much better.

CHAPTER 13

Y ET THAT AT FIRST was the trick that worked—the magic of a clumsy line of trail-worn horsemen pacing forward without anything of a flourish, the action appearing commonplace, as humdrum as farmers riding their work horses to the fields.

For it grew plain that the Indians believed it *was* a trick and could be nothing less. They had snapped at the bait before, and got a mouthful of thorns. They respected the big medicine of this impertinent little foe. It was not conceivable to them that the soldiers intended a plain and desperate face-to-face showdown.

Seasoned Indian-fighters such as Generals Crook and Miles—and Custer, too—had declared ruefully that when the contest lay straight between a trooper and a tribesman, the outcome was seldom in doubt. A lance, an arrow, a lightning knife thrust or slicing tomahawk, and the trooper was mustered out for good. They didn't declare anything on the matter that the Indian didn't know. As for the Pawnee, Shoshone, Crow, they knew every shift and dodge of the white trooper, from observant association as Army scouts. They knew to a hair what the trooper could do and couldn't do, with his heavy gear and arms and laboring horse bought for $125 government money and maybe worth $50 if you threw in the saddle.

The Indians bobbed to a halt, the pale fire of their dust rising about them in the sun, whipping plumes stilled, magnificently deliberate in their suspicious inspection. They wore vermilion daubs on their faces. The tails of their ponies were tied up full of feathers. Their black eyes snapped and their facial muscles twitched frightfully.

Lo, the poor misused savage! Laish thought of the sobbing, purple-passaged penny-a-liners who filled the Eastern newspapers with tearful appeals for justice to the Red Man. They didn't weep for the men who held up a row of brass buttons for the savage to shoot at.

The Indians were watching so, at pause, when Laish halted the slow little line. They watched more keenly when King brought up twenty additional men from the head of the train—an important move, doubtless, in the white men's mysterious trick.

Croshaw, who came with King and the twenty, pushed his undersized mare up close to Laish, and rasped whisperingly in his rage, "There they are—*Gen'ral!* The Injuns you was so sure had quit! There's your goddam gamble! Our cake is dough right here! I never yet seen one o' your gamblin' breed that could play his hand through on the square to the finish! Four-flushers an' mornin' glories an—"

Laish cut a backhand swipe at him. "Get back to the wagons, you! See that they're locked in close corral. All wheels blocked and chained. Pile up everything that'll serve for barricade. Everybody who's got a gun must stand ready. Don't forget to leave a gap open for us when we round in." He stared at the guide. "Now, what were you telling me?"

The blow was a glancing one, and Croshaw didn't bother to touch his cheek where it struck. Nor did he make any move, with either hand. He gazed off at the Indians. His face flared red, but he spoke in his normal tone, remarking sparely that he saw no Apaches yonder.

"Been a fight, and they got whipped off," Laish said. "It was bound to happen. Some big-mouthed Apache talked out of turn at the whisky wagon, or maybe one bunch or the other claimed all the whisky. What a Donnybrook that must have been!"

"Your whisky done it," Croshaw granted. "It held 'em up for a spree an' a scrap. I reckon you've seen an Injun when he's gone through that kind o' party, ain't you? He's cut an' banged up, but he don't even know it—he's crazy mad, mean as a teased rattler, an' he'd murder his mother for a drink. You're lookin' at a thousand of 'em!"

He switched his stare back to Laish. "The only reason I don't feed you my knife, mister, is you should live to see the end o' this! We're in the hole. I don't see no way out. Nor you. I lived through a massacre, once. The Camp Grant Massacre, down in the Aravaipa. You oughta hear the women scream, when they drag 'em off. An' the kids. Scalpin' makes a funny sound, like tearin' canvas. They don't cut it right off, y'know. Just a slash an' a yank. Your scalp oughta look pretty, hangin' on a Pawnee bridle!"

At the head of the dark Indian mass a figure far out in the forefront shook a rifle in the air, shook his swagger war-bonnet of eagle feathers, yelling harangue to eager sub-chiefs and leading warriors of the horde. The figure sat tall astride a large yellow horse. With his every movement a dangling silver disc danced and winked in the sunlight.

"Rasakura," murmured Croshaw. "Tellin' 'em they'll sure count coup on us this trip!"

He trotted his little mare back to the wagons.

A party of about two hundred—the Shoshone section—detached itself from the main Indian body and charged.

It looked like the genuine thing. Shoshones notoriously had a competitive desire to cut in ahead and shine over other tribes when a promising chance cropped up. But it turned out to be a feint, the first in a deadly game, the object being to cut the skirmish line of troopers off from the emigrant train.

The troopers, a long half-mile out from the train, hurriedly shortened their skirmish line, bracing to meet the attack. Wheeling off, the Shoshones left the blue line untouched, then wheeled again, curving in to outflank it and slice in behind it.

King's twenty and Carqueville's dozen raced smartly and headed them off, after a lively crackle of gunfire. Obvious to everybody, though, was the fact that the Shoshones could have swamped them and broken through had they been less wary of a hidden trick. Three more times they stabbed—left, right, and left again, around the flanks of Laish's command—feeling it out, as an expert swordsman would test his opponent before stepping back to plan the decisive death-thrust.

It took on the aspect of an intellectual sport. Back there, the wagons, a circle, the prize. Here, the too-short blue line to defend it, with King's and Carqueville's squads racing to and fro behind the line to fend off the surround. Yonder, the hostile legion, Rasakura's army, watching its Shoshone allies trying to shine. So far, the pawns had all the action on the board. Rasakura would advance his massive master-move as soon as his intelligence told him it would win.

The onlooking Pawnees jeered the Shoshones after the fourth attempt to surround the skirmish line, but by then they knew and the Shoshones knew that there was no hidden trick, no trap; only a bunch of Springfield shooters putting up a forlorn fight, nothing to hide but saddle sores.

In that lull between tentative tests and full assault, Lieutenant King circled around and cantered up to Laish.

"All enemy attacks thrown back, sir," he reported, with his invariably correct salute. "No penetration. My casualties are two killed, five wounded. The enemy losses, I believe, are considerably higher."

Pride then burst through the rigidly conservative armor, and he declared, "The enemy strategy was excellent, but we smashed it! My men fought beautifully. Our Springfields are well served, sir!"

Something grated on Laish's nerves. He searched for it, found it in King's words. *My* men. *My* casualties.

Kind God in heaven, didn't King realize he was speaking of men? Not of numbers. Of men—living men, dead men, hurt men. Did West Point nowadays emphasize only the cold mathematics of war?

Men with broken bones sticking out, crippled for life—good redblooded men like Lybarger and Hoback and the others. *My* casualties! Write them off with a scratch of the pen, send in the requisition for replacements—easier to get than remounts or new equipment, because there was always a cheap and inexhaustible supply of restless Americans, Irishmen, Germans, all kinds, even Englishmen, willing to serve for thirteen dollars a month and the hell of it.

"Sir," King asked, "don't you think that a good rider, on a good horse, might reach Fort Laramie by about midnight?"

It was hardly a question. Rightly, King was proposing the obvious and urgent act, the one that common sense told him should never have been neglected. He could retain his crisply impersonal tone; he could not mask the censure in his eyes.

Laish nodded slowly. "He might, barring accidents. Two

men, better. One to cover the other's rear. Who, King? Who would try it? It's a case for volunteers. Corporal Carqueville would, I think, for one. I would want Askel for the other, but he's gone. Who else?"

"Myself, sir! Four years in the riding academy." King smiled slightly. He did not lack nerve. "I missed cavalry by a fluke. Cavalry was what I wanted."

"Very well. You'd better exchange horses with me. Mine is the better one, I guarantee that. A damned good horse." Dismounting, Laish shocked his injured leg and staggered a step. King was instantly beside him with a steadying shoulder.

Hearing his name spoken, Carqueville had curved in, dismounted, saluted. "Sir?"

"Carqueville—" Laish paused. "Mr. Carqueville," he said, to King's huge astonishment.

A slight trace of what may have been pleasure crossed Carqueville's bone-smooth face. His cool gaze touched on Laish and rose remotely, loaded with tranquil knowledge. He said in a manner precluding any lack of understanding, "Yes, sir." For King's benefit he rattled off casually, "I wish to volunteer, sir, to ride to Fort Laramie—if such be *your* wish."

"Thank you," Laish said. He suspected that Carquevile had also knocked around on the Mexican border, so he said to him, *"Gracias, amigo."*

Carqueville responded graciously, *"Por nada, mi general!"* Meaning it was nothing—a trifling service between gentlemen. Carqueville had courage of the quietly desperate kind that never lost sight of humor.

A long arm of racing pony-riders reached after the two couriers on the instant that the two set off. Another arm whipped frighteningly fast around the wagon train to catch the pair if they should dodge off their course. Laish's skirmish line split out into sections, trying to bend back and delay the Shoshone pursuit of King and Carqueville, to give the pair a head start and a chance, but it was like trying to block an avalanche with brooms.

The firing of the emigrants—hasty shots at the Shoshones flashing by—beat a flatted crackle underneath the wagons. From firearms of many types, the sum of sound matched that of rocks poured down a wooden chute. The emigrants had big old smoothbores, cap-and-ball pistols, long squirrel guns, weapons that their grandfathers had sworn by. No wind blew, and the black-powder smoke hung low and thick to blind the shooters. They blazed away regardless, with a visible score of one—a buck who lost control of his wound-maddened pony and crashed headlong into a wagon.

Failing to halt the Shoshones, Laish's whole command got smeared into scattered groups. The main Indian force under Rasakura seized that opportunity to heave its attack.

Hoback, sticking hard by Laish, kept bugling Recall, until the brassy glitter of his instrument attracted Indian sharpshooting. Some of the younger recruits didn't recognize the call, if they heard it; their blood was up and they fired and galloped futilely after the Shoshones. Some, seeing the start of Rasakura's awesome advance, figured the call meant skin fast for the wagons.

Laish heard the close whicker of a bullet, and its smack. He caught hold of Hoback, who was keeling over out of his saddle. To hold onto him was all Laish could do. He needed help to get Hoback off the open prairie, and it had to come quick or he and the trumpeter were going to be stepped on by Rasakura.

Hoback lay heavily on him, mumbling, "You better go,

sir. I'm—" Blood in his throat clogging the rest of it.

Pepper Troop, with its reinforcements from the flanking files and advance guard, was in the ruck of it again, all spraddled out before the oncoming, firing enemy. The tough-job troop. Horses went down kicking and squealing, men ran afoot to meet those riding to pick them up, and Sergeant Lybarger assembled a mounted bunch and led them right across the thundering face of Rasakura's charge, to Laish.

"We got him! Light for the wagons!"

Grabbing hold of Hoback, and shoving Laish: "Goddammit, here they come!" Unconsidered language; to hell with rank. "*Ho*-lee jeez, they're damn near on us! Run for it!"

Stretched out at full gallop, here and there two men to a horse and another hanging on, running. A man sawing his horse's mouth—that impossible Army bridle-bit, designed by some Washington desk-jockey—to skitter around and go back for his bunkie who crawled with a shattered leg. A farmer kid from Ohio snapping his empty Springfield over and over, shouting blackmouth that he'd never learned at home. This was not recall, nor retreat. This was rout.

Paint-freaked faces of Indians, bobbing into the gunsights and away again, seeming to grin into the kicking muzzles. Reason said it wasn't possible to stop their coming, and fear said you'd never make it to the wagons. If you didn't, with luck the last of it was a white flash without much pain, last words booming from way back in the mind: *Our Father, which art in heaven . . .*

Or, if you were a Carqueville kind of man, a tag of something such as he had quoted one hopeless night: "*Peace be to my sable shroud! Now I am gone . . .*"

They slammed at the gap that was left open for them in

the ring of wagons. There had to be cost, for that ride. Three men cut off, at first count. Three turned back for them. Two fought clear, on one horse.

The troopers streamed through the gap in the circle made by one in-swung wagon. Once inside the corral, they flung off and let their mounts go and ran to the barricaded wagons. Their horses kited about free, raising commotions among the mules, but that didn't break regulations now. The troopers knew without any telling that it was Springfields on the defense line or die. All able wounded were for duty, and some that weren't able for much more than cussing. The in-swung wagon was jammed into the gap, closing the circle. The women filled Christella's medical department, and worked the ammunition detail. They had rigged up a hospital tent, out of wagon-sheets.

The legion of Indians slowed, looking the circle over, inspecting it for weak spots, and came massively on.

CHAPTER 14

LYBARGER BROUGHT LAISH WORD that the Shoshones were already returning from chasing King and Carqueville. He had to yell to make himself heard above the shooting.

"It don't look good for the lieutenant an' Carky, sir. I don't reckon they made it. Fact is, sir, I saw one o' them Injuns comin' back ridin' Carky's horse." Rank smoke from the burned black powder caught in Lybarger's lungs, and he choked and hawked.

"We're low on water, too," he said, spitting. "Them women sure use it up, with their washin'. I could make a canteen do a week, but not them. They want a bar'l a day. Jeez!"

"They won't wait to thirst us out, sergeant."

"No, sir, that's fact. Whole lake wouldn't do us no good now." Lybarger sighted his rifle, fired. He had trouble ejecting the empty cartridge case, and had to dig it out with his claspknife. These old Springfields fouled on every few rounds. His pale eyebrows frowned a straight bar, and creases put a new shape to the crooked blue scar on his broken nose. He scraped the breechblock and slipped in another shell.

"This had to come sooner or later," he said. "We done awful good, sir, to last this long from Fort Taylor."

He meant it wasn't the general's fault, this disaster. He

wanted the general to know it wasn't, in his opinion—if a sergeant's opinion counted for anything with a general. He also conveyed the fatalism of the old soldier—and of the Arab, Askel, with his hushed, *"Mek'toob."* In all races and all tongues it cropped up, especially among men who made violence their trade. What is to be will be. It is written. If the bullet's got your number on it, it'll find you. It had to come sooner or later.

Here was the picture all over again, repeated so often since white-tops first dared to begin pushing out beyond the frontier and go tracking westward across the plains: a caravan corralled at bay, brought to its last stand. Every soldier and emigrant had heard the tales of defeat, among them the grisly one about the Army supply train that fell to red ravagers on this same trail. It had been bound for Fort Laramie, and it put up a stiff die-hard fight. But the tribesmen were too many.

They had branded the wounded with hot king-pins and tossed them into burning wagons. Non-coms were stripped and then dragged to death behind ponies, with ropes. The young officer in command had staged a notably stubborn defense; he had with him his bride, fresh from the East, and was taking her to Fort Laramie, his station. So they spent more time on him, finally cramming his mouth with gunpowder and setting it off. His bride vanished into captivity.

"We've sure made 'em pay!" said Lybarger between shots. "An' they'll pay more yet!"

"Yes," Laish agreed. "But they're willing to meet the price, dammit!"

"They're crazy!" Lybarger grunted. "Kill-crazy!"

More than that, Laish thought. Racial hatred, perhaps, flourishing in the manure of broken promises and forgotten treaties and thoughtless insults. And despair, exasperation. Indians had become convinced that the white man had too many chiefs—boards of solemn commissioners who said one thing, and orders from Washington that said something else before the commissioners even left the country. The white chiefs didn't know the difference between friendly and hostile Indians, either.

Peering over the barricade at Rasakura's confident army, it came to Laish that the poor Indian, the misused savage, was perfectly well able to take care of himself within extensive limits and to beat the hell out of those he disliked, to boot. The Indian's basic error, his crime, was that he craved to hold onto a vast empire for his hunting ground, when the pressure of mankind-at-large insisted that the land should support a million people, or millions.

There again rose that rule of the greatest good for the greatest number; a hard rule to the few, a fair and necessary rule to the many. The history of the world was the history of shifting peoples. The Indian had driven out the previous tenants of this land, no doubt, eons ago when he migrated over the ice sheets from the far Mongolian East. He had to make room now, in his turn, for the next migration.

In the process, he fought back, massacred and tortured the newcomers, but could not halt the great move, the cycle, the turn of the wheel. For it was progress; with all its faults and abuses, its course ran toward some far-off high objective which man could not see and probably would not see for eons yet to come. Wars and savage cruelties could not hold it back. Otherwise, life stood as a wasted miracle, the brainless trick of a cosmic conjurer.

Wagon trains, when well armed and tightly corralled, often had beaten off Indian attacks, and that was the cheering fact that gave emigrants confidence to set out across the continent. And this year the hostile Sioux were quiet. The haughty Ogallalla and ugly Brulé were gone sullenly into hiding, having lost faith in their great war chief, Red Cloud.

But this time the Indian attackers were men who had helped shatter Red Cloud's prestige and drive back the Sioux. They were led by Rasakura and spearheaded by Pawnees, incomparable scouts, proud of their fighting ferocity, and made the more dangerous by their experience in military operations. On all counts it was an outlaw army, as flagrant in guilt as a band of marauding white renegades.

Lifting long lances in rousing encouragement, the sub-chiefs converged inward behind the spear-tip that was Rasakura, leading the charge on his big yellow horse, and the onrushing horde consolidated into one colossal beast— a nightmare serpent splashed with raw colors and slimed in body grease, mouthing one long howl, aiming its lunge at the ring of wagons.

It jarred the ground, and Lybarger's scream, "Fire all!" was an unheard grimace of dirt-crusted lips. But close-spaced spurts volleyed out along the arc of barricade from .50-caliber Springfields and emigrant guns.

Then it became a tumultuous red sea smashing against a reef, and the spume spilling over into the besieged circle. In the strangling thick reek of burned powder a lean face rose between wagons and came thrusting through, long black mane of hair flying, agile brown body a clambering scramble of arms and legs.

Two crooked bars, red and black, striped the Pawnee's cheeks. Red for war, black for death, and he was chanting, "*Tatara kita-vira . . .*" Death-song of the Pawnee—the Pa'ni, meaning Wolf, the name given them by other tribes

167

in recognition of outstanding craft and ferocity and hard-to-kill endurance.

The warrior's blazing glare fastened on Laish, and his arm whipped back a scalp-tasseled lance. Laish fired his pistol at him, feeling his stomach knot, aware of other half-naked shapes breaking over, left and right.

His shot did not miss, he was certain, for he saw the dimpled hole, ringed by the gun-blast spatter. Yet it changed nothing. The Pawnee came on at him, chanting, *"Narutitawe—he-re . . ."*

He tripped the hammer of his pistol again and there was no kick of recoil, no discharge. He jerked aside from the lance, striking at it with the empty pistol. The blade darted under his left arm, in line with his heart, and he closed his arm, clamped down on it. He got his hand on the sleek shaft and wrenched back. The Pawnee fell twistingly against him and was on top as they both fell to the ground, letting go of the lance and snaking his hands swiftly at Laish's throat.

Laish hit him in the face with the gunbarrel, three times. Short, jabbing, scraping blows. The Pawnee rolled his head and after a series of hard little grunts he brought up blood and fell away. The bullet-hole showed high in his chest; it should have finished him at once. The Pa'ni was hard to kill.

The guns continued roaring, but the mad red tide swept on around the barricaded wagons, punching at them, shooting on the run. It rarely satisfied the Indian temperament to concentrate a siege consistently on one spot for long. Young bucks, impatient for personal glory, liked the showy dash and daring foray too well, and the wise old heads couldn't hold them.

Ponies and warriors lay kicking or motionless outside the wagon corral; inside sprawled the broken bodies of eight death-song berserkers who had won personal glory to spare, for they had fought right into the white stronghold and left their mark. Total casualties, soldiers and civilians, amounted to seventeen killed, twenty-three wounded. Five of the dead were members of the Tillotson crew. Tillotson's big freight wagons had borne the brunt of the onslaught.

Encirclement better suited the Indians. Regardless of superimposed army training, they loved their ancient tactical tradition of long arms and streams of horsemen ringing in the enemy. The galloping go-round lent itself perfectly to lightning swoops, individual coups, which multiplied as the noose tightened, until raids clawed unceasingly at the wagon-wall. They struck again and again at the same section where they had made their first full attack. That place seemed to possess a fascination for them.

Lybarger was of the opinion that the Indians were after Tillotson's freight wagons. "Goddam boneheads figger them green wagons is all loaded with booze, like the other'n we left behind for 'em, an' they crave a bracer! Don't you reckon that's it, sir?" He had totally given up addressing Laish in the royally polite and militarily required third-person.

The general very obviously favored a more comfortable kind of camaraderie. The general was a ragged, worn-out scrapper, fighting beside you, and he didn't even notice, and sometimes he called you sarge, like a regular trooper.

"That could be it," Laish said. "But are they such goddam boneheads as that? Seems to me— Look out, sarge! Get that turkey!"

Sergeant Lybarger got the turkey, a Crow warrior swooping in, with a .50 caliber bullet. The Crow jolted off his pony, came crawling on knees and elbows, clutching his knife, and it took another bullet to finish him. "That guy was crazy!" Lybarger said, digging out his empty cartridge case. "Holy be-creest, they're *all* crazy!"

He turned a solemn face to Laish. "I went through the war," he said. "I thought the Rebels was crazy. But these jokers! Jeez!"

"Yes," Laish said. "Courage is the damnedest thing."

The sun sank low and left the welter of battle behind, and still the raids continued, more madly reckless than ever, the circling riders breaking up into groups, discarding organized control, launching fanatic attempts to cut into the ring of wagons. They slacked off only when dusk deepened toward darkness; even then small mobs of them banded up, returned for one more fling, an expression of sheer rage, as if night brought the end of their last chance for this day and they could not bear to wait for next morning.

When the Indians withdrew it was only a short distance. They flung off their sweat-drenched and trembling ponies and dropped to the ground, too spent to clot into their usual camps of tribal divisions and dog-soldier clans. They had shot their bolt for the day. And so had the defenders of the caravan.

In that time of scowling respite, Mignon came to Laish. She found him leaning slumped against a wagon wheel, head bent, eyes closed. "You sent him out!" she accused him. "You sent him out to die!"

With enormous effort he lifted his head and made his peering eyes focus on her. He took note of her tears and of her breaking voice. She held her hands clasped behind her in the attitude of a child facing up to a formidable adult. But in a valley of his mind trailed the roll of names: Vedder, Renehan, Jorgensen, Babcock, Casey, Chacon . . . Names of silent lumps under blankets.

Of none of them was she speaking; no. In all this bloody muck of dying, one man held infinitely more significance for her than the rest put together. She was like that woman crying for a coffin, no room in her grief for thought of anybody else.

"Carqueville volunteered, with King," he said dully to her. "I truly believed he might make it. He was a very fine horseman. And he had brains."

She caught her breath shudderingly, stifling an outburst of sobbing. "Fine in every way! Gentle, and understanding. We—we made plans. I would help him rebuild his life."

He nodded. "I believe you could, yes. And well worth it. What happened? I'm told an Indian was seen bringing back his horse. That is all I know."

"He and King were cut off by the Shoshones. They fought for a little while. Some think King may have got away. Nobody knows. There was so much dust."

"If so, I hope to God he makes it to Fort Laramie tonight!"

"You hope it was King, don't you? Not my man!"

"Your man?" He considered slowly her use of that term. "Why, no. If one of them got clear, I hope it was Carqueville. The better man, in my opinion."

Her staring disbelief did not anger him, as once it would have done. He took a step and laid his hands on her shoulders. "I have no reason to wish Carqueville dead. For your sake, I wish with all my heart that he lives. I'm very fond of you, little Mignon. Always will be. I've carried you in my memory a long time now, you know. The roots are deep. But, frankly, I find I'm not in love with you—not in that special way. I seem to have outgrown it."

Then her overwrought emotions broke out of control. She huddled against him, sobbing, gasping shreds of sentences that were only half lucid.

"Oh, Bart—I'll always love you—be fond of you! He—I love him so, and he loves me and . . . It's real! I've loved others—he knows that. I told him everything. He said—well, he's not an angel, either, and we . . . I think I'm growing up, Bart. It's time! I've been a horrible fool, and I hated to hurt you, and I wouldn't for the world, but I love him and—and—"

"Sure."

She slipped right back to a charming Southern eighteen. "Oh, Bart, Ah just cain't he'p it and that's all!"

"He was—is a damn' good man," Laish said, holding her to him, stroking the nape of her neck, as he would have stroked a frightened kitten. He thought with hopeless regret of the significance of that captured horse led by a Shoshone warrior. "I'd give anything to know he was the one who got clear, if one of them did."

"It could have been, couldn't it? It could have been he!" Unutterable woe pleaded for a straw of hope. "He might have got thrown—perhaps his horse fell. Perhaps he ran to help King, but King was dead, so he took his horse and escaped on it. It *is* possible, isn't it! Isn't it, Bart?"

"It is possible," Laish granted gently. And Mignon nodded eagerly, quick to accept and nurse the tiniest speck of forlorn encouragement.

"Yes, it could have happened that way," Laish said. He felt dried-out and as old as folly. "Yes, Mignon, of course . . ."

In the hospital tent the wounded lay between blankets, not talking, some of them watching earnestly the flame of the single lantern. The flame flickered, reddish and smoky, as the evening wind searched out the gaps under the canvas walls of the makeshift tent and swept in puffs of dust.

They were a bit pale in the face, with a drawn look about the mouth and eyes. They had plumbed the serious side of soldiering. There was no lift in it. No cheers, no admiring onlookers. Only the plainly vigilant emigrant women of Christella's volunteer medical department, with basins and bottles. And the sinister threat of septic poisoning hovering over all.

Trumpeter Hoback lay unconscious. He didn't know the general was paying him a visit, or he maybe would have groped around for his trumpet; it hung close by him, mutely flaunting its ragged bullet-hole and scratches and dents. Somebody had hung it there. Christella, most likely. It was touch-and-go with Hoback. He might pull through, might not.

Next to Hoback lay uncomplaining a trooper whose luxuriant lady-fetching mustaches kept twitching. Shot through the groin with a bitten bullet that splayed. He was worrying if he'd ever be a man again.

On Hoback's other side, a kid kept humming a farm-country tune. He had too-bright eyes that danced and fixed on nothing for long. One of the women stood ready near him.

"His right foot will have to be amputated," Christella whispered to Laish. She moved, placing herself before his sunken, bloodshot eyes. Her voice gentled in pity as she asked, "Why did you come here? My dear, are you punishing yourself?"

He stared blindly through her. The heavy exhaustion crushed all expression from his haggard, blackened face. "A man should see the results of his actions," he said.

"Croshaw is right."

Misunderstanding him, she asked, more gently still, "Lieutenant King is dead, then? Did you trick him into going, to get rid of him? Surely you must know how unnecessary that was."

He raised a hand and let it fall. "No. I take the blame for this. But for that—no. I didn't trick King. I gave him my horse. I hoped he'd get through. I still hope so. Or Carqueville. One of them."

"Without you, this train would have been slaughtered by now," she told him. "It was terribly close to disaster when you reached us and took command. Let us go outside." She led him out of the hospital tent.

Her dress was smeared and stained darkly all down the front, and had the chlorine odor of iodine and carbolic; and he was a broken-down roughneck, a shambling caricature of an officer, having a scruffy odor that was indescribable. They were anything but a romantic-looking pair. The tired women, if they thought anything, perhaps wondered what they saw in each other. Wondered, with morbid speculation, what it was that he found lacking in his beautiful young wife. And mutely decried, with female censure, Christella's morals, as well as her shortsighted folly in not giving encouragement to the handsome young Lieutenant King, a proper gentleman if there ever was one.

Outside, she said to him, "Give yourself credit, as God surely does. You have committed sins in your life, but you have wiped them out in the time that I have known you. I don't think you will commit them again. Even if I thought you would—even if I thought you were an unregenerate blackguard, incapable of redemption—I fear I would still go on loving you."

He reached his hands to her. She came to him readily,

swiftly. He felt her body tremble and tighten in his arms, and press strongly against his. He said, "I love you, Christella. I'll always love you . . ."

Always was a long time. There was only tonight. And that was enough.

CHAPTER 15

SHE STOOD HOLDING HIS HANDS, listening with him, both now growing aware of noises having started up again outside of the barricaded wagon corral. Already the warriors were throwing off their exhaustion, or else fresh ones were on the move.

"You are keeping your father's pistol loaded and ready?"

"Is there no hope at all?"

"There is always hope," he hedged. "In one way that's a bad thing. It could trick you into waiting too long when —if—the time comes you should use the pistol. That would be my blame, too."

Her fingers gripped his fiercely. "Stop thinking of blame!"

He turned to her. "You don't know why help from Fort Laramie hasn't met us before this, do you? Then I must tell you, before you are told by Croshaw or somebody else. It is because I gambled that we were free of the Indians. I deliberately held back any word from going forward to Laramie, because any troops from there would know Pepperis by sight—would know I'm an impostor. I'd be caught, and sooner or later I'd face a firing squad."

"Self-preservation—" she began.

"—Is the first law of nature," he finished for her. "Yes,

I told myself that, too. I told myself—and told you—that I'd get past Fort Laramie, with luck. My game was to stay with the train until almost there. Then quietly slip off—vanish. A change of clothes, somehow, and a shave. Lie up farther along the trail and quietly rejoin the train when it came through. That was my game, my gamble. I risked the whole train on my luck, and luck isn't with me."

She let her hands fall, and bowed her head and whispered, "I must share your blame."

"No! I'm the one who failed to send word—"

"And I am the cause," she whispered. "But for me, you would have sent word. You would have quit the train long ago, while it was safe, and left King in command to meet the troops from Fort Laramie. You had a good horse, and money, and the resourcefulness to make your way anywhere you wished to go—Santa Fe, perhaps. You didn't do it. Because of me. Isn't that so?"

He couldn't deny that, and she said, raising her face, "I know I have your love, as you have mine. But at what a cost! I will not—I promise you I will not wait too long to use the pistol. Make your mind free of that, at least." She turned and hurried back into the hospital tent.

After dark he put out pickets, and the Indians chewed the snuff out of them and chased them back to cover.

For this night the Indians deferred an ancient abhorrence and risked losing their souls to the malign spirits of darkness. To keep their movements the better masked they did without campfires. They formed packs on foot and crept forward, springing surprise forays that strained the defenders' nerves to the edge of collapse. They kept soldiers and armed civilians constantly scurrying from one sudden flare-up to another.

Lybarger, that reliant backbone, a man quietly possessed of a company staff's ubiquity, told Laish straight that the whole show was falling apart.

"They're—I don't know how to say it, sir. High casualties an' low prospects an' no let-up. It's too much, after all they been through. Know what I mean, sir?"

"Played their hand out. Yes, I know." Laish rolled half over and propped himself up on one elbow to look at Lybarger. The sergeant's scarred and broken nose was a mournful hook under unhappy eyes, and only his bristled jaw remained stubborn from tough habit.

"That's it, sir. Played out. But by God they ain't yet layin' off like that Tillotson bunch! Them stinkin' chickens quit ev'ry alarm an' leave us holdin' their damn wagons! It ain't right, sir. If that's the prairie breed, give me barracks birds!"

"Some scum in every stew pot. Tell our men—" Laish paused and breath ran out of him in a long sigh. Who was it said false hope came cheap?

"Yes, sir?"

"Tell them we'll get a rest from these raids before long, if we hold tight. An hour. Two at the most." And he translated Lybarger's look as a skeptical question. "Dammit, man, they can't keep this up all night! They must be as done up as we are. It's high casualties and no let-up for them, too. It's too much for them, as well as us."

"I'm to tell the men that too, sir? As comin' from you, sir?"

"Yes."

The raids did not stop in an hour, nor in two. But not long after midnight they did. The Indians dragged off and lighted their fires beyond rifle range, and *then* the show fell apart. Men at the barricaded wagons simply collapsed in coma-like sleep, their legs and arms twitching as the overtaxed nerves gradually loosened. Somebody shouted urgently, and Laish lay listening for more, but it was only a dreamer.

He was wakened by a hand touching his shoulder. "Take it easy," murmured Croshaw, nimbly dodging. "Set the gun down."

He sank onto his heels and laid a rifle before him on the ground. "Be hell wakin' up this outfit. We got an hour left till light, but they'll be at us 'fore then."

"Think so?"

"The chiefs are having a council, what I could make of it. They got out o' hand yest'day. Won't do it again. You can bet Rasakura's talkin' cold sense into 'em. He's got to make it this time, first crack." Croshaw dipped his chin at the rifle that he had laid down. He said strangely, "See this?"

Laish ran his hand over the rifle. It was sticky with packing grease—a new Henry repeater, sixteen-shot. Army officers carried them, bought out of their own funds, in preference to the single-shot Springfield that was outmoded but not yet supplanted in the ranks. The Tillotson crew was equipped with them. A formidable arm, with its rapid rate of fire.

"Is this one of Tillotson's? It's shop-new, barrel and breech still stuffed with grease."

"Yeah. Never been fired since it was shipped from the factory." Croshaw's faded eyes shone round and luminous. "I been prowlin' through his merchandise. Took a notion the Injuns might be right—maybe he *was* freightin' more firewater in them big green wagons they're tryin' so hard for. But, no, it ain't firewater they're after. It's guns."

His mouth gaped open in silently ferocious laughter. *"Five wagon loads o' guns!* That's his valuable merchandise—for his Green River trade! Sioux trade! You count yourself tricky? Man, how he tricked you out o' searchin' his wagons!"

Laish was sitting up, staring at him, breathing curses.

Croshaw poured out his story. "Enough guns for an army! New repeaters! Ammunition, boxes of it—an' powder an' caps an' lead for reloads! To trade to his Sioux friends, his best customers! What would they do with 'em? Hunt buff'lo? Not on your life!"

"Bigger game! Their favorite old game!"

"Sure. But they'd pay Tillotson first. They're kinda straight, that way. They'd wipe out the other white traders an' leave him a clear field, no competition, an' bring him the loot. He's never got along with other traders. Then Red Cloud, he'd lead 'em out to hunt down Rasakura an' the Pawnees an' ev'ry Injun that served as an Army scout against the Sioux. He holds a big grudge. These fellers know it, don't think they don't! Is it any wonder they're out to catch them green wagons from goin' through?"

"It's—"

"Listen to that!"

The low sound crept to them. Stuttering, repetitive, a breathless agitation of sound wavering up from mumble to imperative growl. Out there somewhere a lean hand thumped the painted skin of a war drum, commanding warriors to arise, prepare.

Laish said, slapping the new rifle, "The main objective! Andy Pepperis knew it had to be something big, something definite, not a wildcat impulse, to make them turn on him like that."

"Big enough," agreed Croshaw, dispassionately. The galloping boom of the Indian drum seemed to stamp out altogether his spark of anger. "I oughta smelled it, but damned if I did. Hell, it was me spoke for Tillotson, when he asked to join this train, come to think of it. An' it was me said *you* done wrong! I bet you'd like to bust my neck now, for sure."

"Some other time. D'you know any of Rasakura's mob?"

"Scores. That don't signify nothin'. It's like most us whites, we blame all the Injuns for what some of 'em do. Injuns are the same about us. Them fellers helped the white sojers beat back the Sioux an' open up this trail. They kinda look for a leetle gratitude, but what do they see? White men's wagons carryin' guns to their sworn blood-enemies. Train o' whites gives 'em protection. White sojers, fightin' to get the wagons through. They figger the white men are all in cahoots to sell 'em out to the Sioux. It wouldn't be the first dirty deal they ever got. No—I don't count no friends there, if that's your meanin'! Nor no talkin' acquaintances. They jest ain't in the mood to listen to *no* white rubbish!"

"Where's Lybarger?"

"I'll scout him up for you."

"Tell him we've got one more job for Pepper Troop, will you? A wagon detail, sort of, tell him. And ten men who can ride."

"All right, Gen'ral."

By the time they had caught and laced up the mule teams, and cut the five green wagons out of line, dawn was a bursting fire spraying the eastern sky and all the drums had gone mute. Gray faces, pinched and desolate, stared from the barricade; morning brought their blackest hour.

The hostiles waited, more than ready. The two horns of their half-moon formation kept edging forward, impatient for the attack signal from tall Rasakura sitting his yellow horse well to the front and center like a brigade commander on parade.

Tillotson did not put in an appearance. That fear-haunted adventurer had sniffed the approach of exposure, Laish guessed, and ducked somewhere out of sight. His crew had quit the wagons again, and now their behavior all along became more understandable. They knew the perilous nature of that freight. Knew exactly what Rasakura was after. Knew he wouldn't give up till he got it or died.

According to Croshaw's reckoning the Indian attack was overdue. Set to be sprung in total force twenty minutes back, it hung fire only on a burr of curiosity. The Indians watched narrowly the activity at the wagons, the distinctive green freight wagons that stood for the white man's perfidy. Rasakura, outstanding star in the great dark crescent of warriors, held his rifle crosswise on his saddle, refusing to fling it up for the charge till the rising sun should unriddle the doings of the whites.

As in studying an opponent's reaction to a one-card draw, across the vast table Laish studied that rigid brooding statue. Rasakura would not be stampeded into a bull-head boner; he had failed before and let the young men's errors do grave injury to his prestige; this next move he would make with the rigorous precision of a chess master.

"Pull out!"

Each driven by a trooper, another riding alongside with a led horse, the five wagons pulled out and away from the circle and opened a break that horsemen thirty abreast could have galloped through. They tracked deliberately on after Laish, like four-wheeled jumbos marching in line. Witless elephants serenely plodding to nowhere. Sunrise revealed them, wiped them clean of flummery, and that was good; that was well timed. The Indians had to see this clearly and realize its consequence.

The dark crescent swayed and raised a din. They were shouting now, screaming to be let loose to capture the five wagons. The yellow horse tossed its head. Rasakura sat immobile, watching, waiting: *There is time, young men. They can never escape now.*

"Far enough!"

The five wagons stood as far from the corralled train as they did from the screaming Indians. They formed one point of an equilateral triangle when the drivers hauled in. The tailgates of the wagons hung open. Noise from the train was no echo of the Indian turbulence. People back there shouted in a different fashion, urgently, as if sighting something that Laish and the ten troopers had not yet seen, and were trying to call attention to it.

Laish reined around and sang out to the driver of the foremost wagon, "All right, on your horse and back to the train! Don't tie those lines—throw them loose!"

The driver jumped down, dropping the lines, and legged into his saddle. He and his horse-holder hesitated, watching Laish, unwilling to leave him out here alone. Laish waved them off, and rode around to the rear of the wagon; he fished out matches and bent over the open tailgate.

It had to be done swiftly, with sureness, while the troopers raced off back to that yawning break in the corralled train and while Rasakura's head-feathers fluttered in motion. Between the most careful preparation and the accomplishment lurked unforeseen trifles that could prevent success. A misplaced twist of rag—a spark that died or else flared up too fast in a wisp of breeze—ornery mules that would bolt at a sneeze and yet wouldn't budge for thunderbolts. Matches whose heads broke off maddeningly, and others that wouldn't burn in hell with a blowtorch. The dumb cussedness of common things.

The process called for hat-slapping and booting the teams to get them irascibly running, driverless, across the plain. It had to be done five times with methodical haste, the mind and the senses concentrated upon the task in hand and disregarding everything else. When the last of the five wagons got off, Laish lit out for the train.

Croshaw's thin squawl was needling through the up-roar: "They're comin', Gen'ral—they're comin'!"

The short measure of time, overcrowded, refused space for rational reckoning. Clogged thought forced an evasive outlet, and in recollection Laish found himself talking again with Brigadier General Andrew Pepperis in the wrecked army ambulance; the dawn sun had been rimming the east then as it was doing now.

"To Oregon. Nobody knows me there."

Well, it had seemed a good move at the time. An expedient, not at all impossible to execute. His life was one expedient after another.

"We all have to pay our toll, one way or other, which-ever way we go."

How trite, and how true. One of the sayings that such a man as Andy Pepperis would use and re-use until its meaning, for him, wore down like an old coin, and the listener boredly discounted it. Yet its verity remained as mint-sharp as ever, and some day the listener remembered and re-appraised it.

"Women and children in that emigrant train—or have you changed so much?"

"Not that much, Andy."

A foolish question and a foolish answer. Did any man ever really change? Rub off the tarnish, or scrape off the bright paint, as the case might be, and the original metal was still there; usually an alloy, with more or less brass.

He shut off that outlet. What the hell, he was arguing with a dead man. Bad sign of overstrain or something. Andy was gone. Soldier's farewell and a big name for the record. After a while only a few old bowlegs living would remember him, over their hot grog. Pepperis? Tugging at their drooping white mustaches. Let's see, wasn't he killed in that queer affair on the Oregon Trail? Sure—and Department had fits over the crackpot rumor that his ghost went marching on up the Platte in command of some juniper infantry from the Fort Taylor disaster.

And there rode the feathered devil who murdered him. The red chief who slew the white chief. The brooding fool who figured Pepper Andy had been marching west to take command of troops protecting the route for gun shipments to the hated Sioux. He had learned of the guns in the green wagons, and put two and two together and made it a dozen. A little knowledge certainly was a dangerous thing.

Let him catch up with the runaway wagons careening off yonder. Let him catch the grand prize, the cause of all this death and bloodshed. No way to prevent him now, anyhow.

Croshaw met Laish at the wide break in the corralled train. "They're comin'!" he squawled again; and Laish, sliding off his hard-breathing horse, touched a look on him and then turned to watch the Indians.

The big yellow horse ran powerfully, far out in front of the rest. Rasakura had not given any signal to charge. He had simply kicked the horse and shot forward, and gained a flying start. The time being right, and all fair ahead, this was his move. The five driverless wagons were free prizes, abandoned ships staggering down the wind, defenseless, heavily loaded and carrying the richest of all possible cargoes—new firearms and ammunition, source of power, means of defiance.

Rasakura had to be first to reach them. No young men should pass the chief in his mighty moment of victory. A matter of pride, of clinching a great prestige.

Splendidly he curved in on the foremost runaway wagon. He leaped, and left the yellow horse running loose. For a little while he could not be seen from the train. All five wagons swayed, their stampeded teams sheering off from the Indian mob quartering after them, churning up dust, and formed a spaced column on left oblique. Roughness of ground broke the column ragged, two wagons falling behind, two diverging widely, one rocking ahead.

Rasakura reappeared, atop the leading wagon. He spun a new rifle high in his right hand, like a conjuring drum major—a brandished trophy, to let his people know that these were the wagons they had fought for, and that he had won them. Not braggadocio, that, but simply an expression of correctly proud self-esteem. As correct, and well-earned, as a cavalryman's swagger.

The trophy he hauled low with his left hand was a man, the body of a man.

Croshaw murmured in Laish's ear, "Tillotson. He catched me prowlin' through his wagons. I had to knife him. Left him there on his valuable goddam merchandise." In a louder tone he began saying, "Dust in the west—"

For half the space of a heartbeat there wasn't a sound. The leading wagon, with Rasakura on top whirling the new rifle in a last flourish, bucked twistingly, bursting its stakes and bows, splintering into fragments.

Then the roar raced out and shook the air, and a huge pudding of dirty blue smoke shed bits of wood and canvas and broken rifles and crackling ammunition boxes that shot themselves asunder like giant jumping firecrackers. Right in the shattering echo of it the second blast came, followed more slowly by the third. The last two wagons exploded almost simultaneously.

There remained nothing then, at last, but the long pall of silent smoke on the prairie, and the debris strewn all around for half a mile. And five holes scooped in the ground, resembling dry buffalo wallows. One mule, hurled a hundred feet, kicked slowly, by some miracle still tenuously attached to a raveling thread of life. It had been good black powder, caps, tested ammunition. The guaranteed best. For the Sioux.

For nobody. For a terrific display of fireworks, blowing Rasakura to bits, leaving his people to ponder on the ironic thought that they had probably ridden and fought for hundreds of miles for nothing. The white man had shown that he placed no value on the guns; by the gesture of destruction he proved it. There was nothing left to fight about.

"There's the end of that!" Laish muttered. And then, remembering, he looked at Croshaw beside him. "What's that you said? Dust in the west? The west?"

"They're comin', yeah. Climb up on a wagon an' see for y'self. It'll take 'em some time yet to get here, though."

Laish dragged himself up onto the nearest wagon, and Lybarger handed him a pair of battered field-glasses. The dust in the west was a hump like a distant hill seen through heat waves, unstable and vagrant, underscored with a dark stroke that thickened perceptibly and steadily. The relief from Fort Laramie was hitting a fast clip; there would be spent mounts and a crop of saddle blisters after that long, hard ride.

Croshaw said, "The lieutenant's a right salty rider for a doughfoot. He made it!"

Mignon heard that, for she had come hurrying, holding her skirts, and was looking up at Laish on the wagon. For her benefit Laish answered, "Carqueville, more likely,

I think."

She nodded in that eager, grateful way. "So do I! I know it! I—I feel it!" Woman's intuition, compounded of prayerful wishing and a kind of occult faith in the power of optimistic belief. Croshaw pulled at his nose embarrassedly.

Laish swept the field-glasses to the drifting smoke of the explosions, and on around. The Indians were leaving.

The reckless ferocity of the renegade tribes was bled out. They had got enough. Rasakura was gone with the many dead, and gone too were the guns and the gun-running trader. Laramie was coming. The appalled red mind turned belatedly to the future, to the months that must come in unhappy hiding and flight from the white wrath: the payment and penance for crime. The warriors seeped off in driblets, already the sub-tribes dividing, breaking up the legion, shunning one another.

Laish backed down off the wagon, awkwardly because of his stiff leg. Somebody helped him, and on the ground he turned and, finding Christella beside him, tried to smile to her.

She asked, "How much time?"

"About an hour, perhaps. Kill their horses, the rate they're coming. Must have heard the blasts." He took her hands in his and bowed to her. "I'll say good-by to you now."

But the jaunty toughness came unstuck, and he said wretchedly, "I wish I could've got past Laramie! With you—in Oregon—we'd—or any damned place—"

"My father's clothes are still packed in his trunk," she interrupted, as briskly businesslike as a quartermaster sizing up a recruit for issues. "They'll fit. He was a big man, like you. Come with me!"

He rode through the dissolving smoke, a man wearing a

black broadcloth suit and white shirt and plain black hat. His mount was the fine sorrel horse that had been Tillotson's; he had thanked Croshaw for it. As Croshaw pointed out, the fresh sorrel could walk away from anything the Laramie relief sent after him, and carry him to where he was going.

"Y'oughta strike ol' Kit's trail t'morrer. Southwest, mind, then south down straight to Santa Fe. It's a real good gamblin' town, wide open. Good luck to you"—Croshaw grinned—"Gen'ral!"

"Thanks. *Adios!*"

A mile beyond the smoke he reined the sorrel full around to halt, for a long look back through Lybarger's field-glasses that he had forgotten to return. God's name, Fort Laramie must have sent every able cavalryman in its garrison. And not one solitary hostile left for them to fight. Sore bunch of bowlegs there.

A horseman broke out from just behind the officers at the head, scandalously irregular, and spurred on forward. He dashed like mad to a girl running from the train to meet him, and whirled around her and dismounted and caught her in his arms. No mistaking that slim trooper. *I think it will be all right, Mr. Carqueville!*

The field-glasses moved on, ranging over the wagons, searching for a particular one, and soon finding it. A scrap of white, a handkerchief, or more likely a clean piece of bandage, fluttered in a waving hand.

He snatched off his hat and waved in response, though doubting that she could see it at that distance in the smoky, dusty air. But she knew he had the field-glasses and would be stopping to look back. Then the Laramie relief trotted around the train, raising a blinding dust, and he swung the sorrel and rode on.

Santa Fe, hell! "With a shave, you won't know me," he

had told her when they parted, and he had held her to him for a brief moment. "Somehow, some day—not too far off, either—I'll get there to Oregon, where *nobody* knows me. Dear girl, I swear it!"

She took his dirty, bearded, haggard face in her hands and kissed him. "I shall be waiting," she told him. "And I will know you. Ten miles off, I'll know you. Please don't make me wait long."

Santa Fe, hell. Oregon or bust!

OTHER FIRST EDITIONS NOW ON SALE